WILD BOY

James Lincoln Collier

T 25014

MARSHALL CAVENDISH • NEW YORK

Library of Congress Cataloging-in-Publication Data
Collier, James Lincoln, 1928-
Wild boy / James Lincoln Collier.— 1st ed.
p.   cm.
Summary: Twelve-year-old Jesse runs away from home
and tries to survive on his own in the nearby mountains.
ISBN 0-7614-5126-9
[1. Mountain life—Fiction.] I. Title.
PZ7.C678 Whk 2002
[Fic]—dc21
2001047610

The text of this book is set in 13 point Bembo.
Book design by Constance Ftera
Printed in the United States of America
First edition
1 3 5 6 4 2

For Jackson, Slater, and Amanda

Chapter One

There was a place where a rock outcropping stuck out of the side of the mountain. Nothing grew there and you could see for miles across the prairie down below. I don't know how many miles —twenty, fifty, maybe a hundred for all I knew. You could see the river wandering through the grass like a brown snake wriggling across the prairie, and beside it the little town where I come from, and not much else— lazy clouds slipping across the blue sky, a few clumps of trees here and there by a sinkhole where there was water. Not much else. The town was maybe ten miles away. I knew, because I walked it more'n once.

But sometimes there'd be people down there, maybe a wagon train of overlanders heading for Oregon, maybe a couple of fellas riding off somewheres, maybe a few Indians racing through the prairie grass on their ponies. I liked going there when I felt lonely, just lie on the warm rock with the sun on my back and see what was going on. Sometimes I'd lie there for the longest time watching a wagon train wind along the river churning up a cloud of yellow-brown dust that rose up and up into the sky, until the wagon train disappeared in the north and I couldn't see it no more.

I was low in mind right then. Hadn't of been able to scare up hardly anything serious to eat for three days. Some wild strawberries I come on in a little clearing, and a fair-sized turtle that was laying on a rock in the sun. Turtles don't have no sense. The strawberries wasn't quite ripe but I et 'em anyway. The turtle was pretty good, but there was blame little to him. I was still mighty hungry as I lay on the warm outcropping, pressing my belly on the rock so as to make it seem less empty.

There wasn't much to see this time, just a couple of fellas loping along on their horses. One of 'em had a buck slung over the rump of his horse. I figured they must of come up to the mountain hunting, to have some fun for theirselves, and was heading back to town to cook up a venison steak. I wondered: was they old pals that liked doing things among themselves? Was one of them a newcomer out here, and this other fella took him out hunting to be friendly? I always liked making up ideas about people I seen down on the prairie, was they this or that?

Still, I wasn't about to go back down there and say hello to them. As far as I was concerned them people could have the town, the prairie and all of that. I had enough of people to suit me for a while. They wasn't no damn good. I couldn't go back there, anyways, for what I did to Pa. But even if I couldn't, I wouldn't of. But oh my, I was hungry.

Still, I was up in the mountains where I always wanted to be, and I was bound and determined I was going to stay there. Them mountain men come into our store from time to time for stuff—powder and shot, new knife when they lost the old one, pants, flour, shoes. Generally they come down every two or three months when they have a load of fur to take to the trading post aways down the river from the town. Pack the skins down out of the mountains on their back, and pack a load of stuff from the store back up into the mountains. Oh, they was something to look at, hair down over their ears, beards all scraggly where they hacked at them with a skinning knife, clothes torn and patched. They looked so hard and fierce, game for anything and wouldn't take nothing from nobody. I couldn't get my eyes off them.

Then they'd go around to the barber for a shave and a haircut, and when they come back you wouldn't recognize it was the same fella. They'd pick out some new clothes off Pa's shelves, go out into the backyard to change, and give Pa their old clothes to burn.

Then like as not they'd sit around the store on a barrel and tell stories: about fighting a bear with a skinning knife, about getting lost in a snowstorm and only saved theirselves by falling into a cave by mistake, about dancing with the Indians and having the Indian girls fall in love with them. Oh, I admired them so. Wasn't nothing I ever wanted to be more'n a mountain man.

But it wasn't all glory. I only been up there two, three weeks and I found that out already. You went hungry a lot of times, cold and wet if you got caught out in a rainstorm two miles from home, and scared often enough when a deer jumped out of the brush and shot across in front of you, or a mountain jack began to holler off in the distance. But there wasn't no way I was going to quit. I'd die first. Couldn't go home, anyways.

I lay there on the rock, trying to think of the sun on my back instead of the ache in my gut, watching them fellas ride into town with the deer, talking amongst theirselves. Leastwise, I supposed they was talking about theirselves. Maybe they wasn't, maybe they was just riding along silent thinking their own thoughts. Didn't seem likely, though. Seemed more likely that a couple of fellas who'd just got theirselves a buck would have been talking amongst theirselves. How this one see it first through the trees, and how the other fella took a shot and only got it in the rump and it took off on them, and how they chased it for ten blame miles it seemed like, following the trail of blood until the buck kind of run out of steam and they cornered it against a rock wall. And the one fella who seen it first joshing the one who'd got it in the rump, saying, "I always knew you was blind, Smitty; either that or palsied." Something like that.

Anyway, if it would have been me and Charlie Williams, and we got ourselves a buck, we wouldn't of been riding along silent, thinking our own thoughts. We'd of been joshing each other good. That Charlie, he was mighty frisky, always joshing and cutting up, and wanting to take a chance on something. Slip into Widow Wadman's pantry for a chunk of her blueberry pie when we seen her set off for church. Something, anything to keep things stirred up. Oh, we'd of been joshing if that'd been us. Me and Charlie was best friends —had to be, the only kids our age in that little town. But then Charlie died on me. Nine years old. Took sick of something and lay in bed for a week. I went over everyday to visit with him. It cheered him up to see me, and he'd talk about what we was going to do next—build ourselves a raft and float down the river, go trapping for muskrats and get rich from the skins, such stuff. About the fifth day I realized he wasn't making no sense, babbling away about giants and pygmies. I knew he was a goner. I couldn't stand it no more. I went out into Charlie's barn, lay down in the hay, and cried until I couldn't cry no more—wasn't no more tears left. I went on home and the next morning Pa told me that Charlie passed in the night. Pa was soft with me for a couple of days after that, but it didn't help much. I ached for him, until I slowly got over it and didn't think about him but just once in a while.

Seeing those men with the buck walking amongst theirselves brought it back. Oh, we'd of had fun if it'd been me and Charlie Williams up there in the mountains.

Then I said, Jesse, you can't let yourself think about them things—what if this, what if that. You got to stop these things circling around in your head all the time, Jesse. How was it Pa put it? You got to be hard on yourself or you ain't going nowhere. Not that Pa was going anywhere, but he was hard on himself and everyone else, too. Paddled my rump often enough until I got too big for it, although I deserved it a good half the time, when I lost hold of myself and started throwing stuff out the windows and such. But the other half the time I didn't deserve it.

Pa had his good side, though. Cooked our meals regular. I never went hungry with Pa, I can say that. Nor raggedy neither. He wouldn't stand for me looking raggedy, and if he didn't have a new pair of pants or shirt my size in the store, he'd take out Ma's old sewing box and sit there squinting and frowning and cursing, jabbing hisself with the needle until he'd got me patched up. Oh, you had to laugh when you saw Pa hunched over my old shirt, squinting and jabbing hisself as he sewed on a button or hitched the shirt pocket back on where I'd ripped it wrestling with Charlie Williams. You had to say that for Pa: he done what he could for me. I hoped to God he wasn't dead. I shuddered. That last time I seen him laying on the floor he was breathing. Wasn't bleeding a whole lot neither. But still, maybe he was dead.

I shuddered again and to take my mind off it I twisted my head around to look back at the trees rising up the mountainside. Oaks, mostly, some maples, and here and there where the soil was specially thin and rocky, hemlocks, some of them a hundred feet tall I reckoned, their tops tipped sideways, shining dark green in the sun.

A little breeze come up. It felt good on my back and I lay back down on my stomach and looked down at the prairie. Them two fellas was a good way off, still moving along through the prairie grass. The breeze come down off the mountain, and ran across the prairie grass, bending it over like a hand brushing through a tawny cat's fur. I knew what was going to happen, because it always did when I seen the wind bending a field of tall grass like that. I lay there kind of frozen, and here come that memory and the bad feeling that always come with it. Knots grew in my belly, my muscles clenched, my head got tight and achy. I shook my head to get rid of the memory, but it stayed, eyes closed or opened.

What I remembered was being in a shed, barn maybe. Left there by myself. Five years old, about, and had a shovel and a bucket to play with. The door to the shed was open, and through it I seen a field of tall grass—hayfield, I reckon—sun shining on brown grass, and the breeze bending it over. At the far side of the field was a patch of trees—we didn't have nothing like a real woods out there on the prairie, but there was patches of trees in places along the river. Something was going on in that patch of trees that was giving me a real bad feeling. I was just a little kid, and didn't have much sense about anything. All I remember is raising up that toy shovel like it was a gun and pointing it towards that patch of trees. *Bang*, I said. That's all I remember of it, except that after a while Ma was there, holding me.

For the life of me, I couldn't remember what that memory was about. Couldn't call to mind what I seen in that patch of trees that gave me such a bad feeling. But all I had to do was see the wind bend a field of grass like a hand running through cat's fur, and it always took me that way. Was it some kind of dream I had once and couldn't get rid of? I didn't think so, but I wasn't sure.

Suddenly I realized I was kneeling up on the rock outcropping, cramp in my stomach and my face wet with sweat. I wiped off my face with my sleeve and waited for the cramps to pass. When they was done I stood up. Jesse, I said, you got to get yourself something to eat before you go crazy.

I thought about the traps. The last time I done it I promised myself I wouldn't do it no more. It wasn't right. But blame it, I was almighty hungry. Couldn't remember being so hungry. There might be something in the traps.

They belonged to one of the mountain men who had a cabin around the corner of my mountain from my lean-to, and a little higher up. He was going for fox, wolf, bobcat, whatever he could get. It was for the skins— nobody'd eat a fox or a bobcat unless they was driven to it mighty hard. I come across the trapline a little while after I first left home and come up into the mountains. I hunted around until I found his cabin. Blame sight nicer than my lean-to. It had a real chimney, a couple of oilpaper windows. I didn't have no windows, just a row of dead logs I dragged up and leaned against a rock wall. I laid branches over the logs to keep the wind and rain out. Dry enough in there for now, but it

12

wasn't going to be no blame good once the weather turned cold. I envied the mountain man his cabin.

I was curious about him, anyway. Who was he, and how did he come to be up there in the mountains, and did he get sick of people the way I done? Was it the same with him as it was with me? Not that I was about to strike up an acquaintance with him. But even so I was curious, and two or three times I circled around the mountain so as to come out a couple of hundred feet above his cabin, and lay there behind a tree in a hemlock grove, smelling the sweet, sharp hemlock smell and watching him split kindling for his fire, skin out a fox, bring up a leather bucket of water from the spring below his cabin. Young fella in his twenties. Had a big black beard and black hair down to his shoulders. I reckoned he hacked it off from time to time to keep it out of his way. Oh, it wasn't like I was looking to make his acquaintance or nothing, but I liked watching him.

I had a blame good reason for staying clear of him, anyway, for by now I took stuff out of his traps twice. Fawn once and another time some kind of wild dog that had run off from somewheres.

Oh, I shouldn't have done nothing like that and I'd of given the pelts back if I dared, for it was the pelts he was interested in. But I was blame hungry both times and couldn't help myself. Well, was I going to do it or not? Maybe if I held out a little longer I'd rouse up something. So I went back down the mountain a ways to where there was a deer trail, climbed up into an oak tree where I had luck before, and set there, waiting. But the whole time my stomach was twisting and bubbling so loud I figured it'd warn off any animal within earshot. All I could think of was a nice piece of venison hot and chewy in my mouth. Finally I couldn't stand it no more. I climbed down out of the oak and went on up the mountain to where the trapline was.

He'd run it not far from where a deer trail crossed over a little stream. All kind of animals was in and out of a place like that. Even as I was coming up to it I could hear some kind of yipping. I come on until I was a hundred feet away and lay down on the dead leaves. There was movement over there, and a lot of snapping and snarling. I began to slide forward, keeping a sharp eye out for the mountain man's traps, for of course they was hid in leaves and dirt. If you stuck an arm in one of them it'd hurt mighty good—break your arm like as not.

As I got closer I could see that he'd got a fox. Baited the trap with a fresh deer bone or some such. I didn't much like the idea of eating a fox. Never et one, nor heard of anyone eating one. Indians, maybe. They ate snakes, beetles, whole lot of stuff a white man wouldn't eat. It made me kind of queasy to think of eating a fox. But I didn't have no choice—if I could eat wild dog I could eat a fox, I reckoned.

But I wasn't going to eat it until I killed it. I couldn't risk a shot—if that fella was anywhere near he'd be on me in a minute. I looked around and by and by I found a couple of good-sized rocks. They'd do. I slipped forward some more until I wasn't ten feet from the fox. He turned and snarled at me, a real ripper. Oh my, he was angry. "Don't you fret," I said to him. "You'll be out of your misery pretty soon." I raised up onto my knees and lifted the rock high to bring it down on the fox's head. Just then a voice not more'n twenty feet behind me said, "Drop it, son."

Chapter Two

I dropped the rock, stood up, and turned around. Behind me the fox went on yipping and snarling—it had its own problems and wasn't much interested in mine. The mountain man's eyes were blue, and even though his beard was cut off uneven and his hair curled around his ears, he'd taken the trouble to keep hisself tidy and clean—trousers patched at the knees where they was worn through, hair combed back even if it was long. But he had the gun leveled at me. "I figured all along it was you," he said.

I didn't know what kind of a fella he was and I was plenty scared—heart pumping, legs shaky, sweat on my face. I didn't say nothing. There wasn't nothing to say—he caught me dead to rights.

"You realize I could shoot you where you stand, drag you up to the mountain, and in two days there wouldn't be nothing left of you but hair?"

That was so. The animals would chew a body up mighty fast and the crows take what was left over. "Well, if you're going to do it, do it," I said. I didn't want him thinking I cared about being alive or dead. "No point in wasting all day over it."

He looked at me for a minute. "Blame hard for a kid, ain't you?"

"I ain't no kid," I said. "I'm coming up for thirteen."

"They said there was a kid gone wild up here. A fella said they seen you skulking around."

It took me by surprise that anyone seen me. I didn't like the idea of it, that people was taking an interest in me. It wasn't none of their blame business. "I ain't skulking. I got as much right up here as anyone."

"That don't give you the right to open another man's traps."

"I was near starved to death." I wasn't so scared no more, for it sounded like he was going to give me a ripping and let it go at that.

He slung the gun under one arm where he could get at it easy. The sun coming down through the oak trees shone on the trigger and trigger guard where the metal was worn bright. "You must have been starved to think of eating a fox. Whyn't you come and ask me for something to eat? I'd of given it to you."

Why hadn't I? It seemed easy enough now that he put it that way. "I don't like to be beholden to nobody. That ain't the way I am." The fox was still snapping away behind me, and I felt sorry for him, but we was in the same fix.

"Better'n stealing out of a man's traps. If you can't take care of yourself up here in the mountains, better get your tail back on home."

I could see he was right about that. If I went on stealing

from traps they was bound to get together and shoot me sooner or later. I didn't say anything.

"What're you going to do when winter comes and there's snow three feet over your head?"

I still didn't say anything. I hadn't thought that far ahead. I hadn't thought much about anything—just lost hold of myself, went after Pa, and ran off into the mountains. "I don't know," I said.

He didn't say anything. Then he said, "Stand aside."

I jumped to one side and before I hit the ground he shot the fox. The yipping suddenly stopped and the sound of the shot echoed through the forest. "Don't you try to make a run for it while I load up. I got legs a lot longer than yours." He started to reload the gun.

I thought about making a run for it, and took a quick look over my shoulder to figure out where to run to. He seen me do it—should have known he would. "Stay where you are," he said. He finished reloading—didn't take him but twenty seconds. "Open up that trap and take that animal out. You got practice enough at it."

I tromped the trap catch. It fell open and I picked the fox out of it. He'd got it clean in the head, saving the pelt. "What do you want me to do with it?"

"You want something to eat, don't you? Carry it up to my cabin whilst I keep an eye on you."

I gave him a look. "You don't have to do me no favors." Right away I wished I hadn't of said that, for I was hungry as could be.

"I didn't say I was doing you no favors. I said I was going to feed you up so's you'd stay out of my traps for a couple of days."

I didn't believe that, but this time I managed to keep my mouth shut about it. "Which way?"

He pointed, and we set off through the forest, me carrying the dead fox, him coming along behind with the gun slung under his arm. It was a good piece over to his cabin, mile maybe, for he'd set up the trapline far enough from the cabin so's he wouldn't scare animals off. He built the cabin in a clearing where the mountain dipped down a little. I never figured out why you had clearings in forests, but you did. Soil too thin for trees in such places, I reckoned. Something. But you got those clearings where the sun come in and grass grew. He'd have some light in a place like that, and be out of the wind.

His spring was fifty feet down the slope. Real nice setup. Grass tall enough to graze a horse if he had one. Oh, it was a nice setup all right: chopping block he sawed out of a maple trunk, with an axe thunked in it; big turtle shell two feet across set on another block he could use for washing—hisself along with the dishes; circle of stones for a fireplace, with a grill perched up over it; a wall of firewood stacked up against one side of the cabin neat and tidy. I wished I had a setup as tidy as that. I didn't have no axe, to start with, and had to be content with picking up fallen branches for firewood.

I could see now that wasn't going to do for winter.

"You think you can make a fire without setting the woods ablaze?" he said.

"What makes you think I couldn't?"

He laughed. "Sore as a boil about everything, ain't you? Well, set to it while I skin this animal out and mebbe we'll have some dinner."

I took out my knife, cut some shavings off a little piece of hemlock that was lying there, knocked some sparks onto the shavings from my steel, and blowed on the sparks real easy until the shavings flared up. I added some twigs, and by and by I had a nice fire going. I'd hardly got the shavings glowing when he had the skin off that fox, just as neat as could be, like he was taking a shirt off a baby. It didn't take him three minutes—I never saw such a handy thing before. Then he went into the cabin and came out in a minute with some things. And presently he was kneeling by the fire holding a big skillet with a slice of ham in it as big as the pan. Tucked up against the fire was a covered bucket with a bunch of biscuits in it. When the smell of ham and biscuits began to rise up it was all I could do to hold myself still. My mouth was watering so much I like to drowned. But there wasn't no way to hurry a fella like that. So I sat there with my arms around my knees, pulling them up close to my belly so as to quiet the rumblings, and waited. But he knew what I was thinking, for he gave me a look and said, "We're getting there. I can't make these here biscuits cook no faster than they want to."

But I was already thinking of something else. "Who was it you said seen me up here?"

"Why everybody seen you, the way you was racketing around like a chicken with its head off. I reckon I was the only one who didn't." He gave me a look. "But I had good reason to know you was around."

I went red. Here I thought I was slipping around through the woods slick as a fox, and all the while the mountain men was on to me. "I didn't see nobody. How come they seen me?"

"You ought to keep it in mind that these here woods ain't as empty as they look. For one thing, you got Indians coming and going. They don't live up here, life's easier for them down on the prairie—or it was until them overlanders starting coming through, trampling down the grass and scaring off the buffalo. But they come up to hunt sometimes."

"Who else?" I didn't like the idea that the woods was full of people. I wanted to be up here alone by myself.

He shrugged, and turned the piece of ham over with the fork. The most beautiful smell rose up off it. "Can't say. There's two or three fellas around here. They come and go. See a fella for a while, then you don't see him, then a year later he's back."

"Which was the one who told you about me?"

He looked at me. "What if I said it wasn't none of your business?"

I tried to look him straight in the eyes, but I couldn't, and looked down. "Well, I reckon it ain't."

"No it ain't," he said. "But I'll tell you anyways. It's a fella called Billings. Has a cabin northwards on the next mountain. Maybe eight, ten miles up that way. He don't like the idea of you being up here at all. Not at all. Said you was scaring all the game off, making a mess of things generally, and would get in a fix sooner or later and have to be rescued."

"Why'm I scaring off the game worse than anyone else?"

"Oh, I don't know as you are. Mebbe a little casual traipsing around hither and yon is all. He don't like kids very much, I reckon. Specially one running wild in the mountains. Kind of a scratchy fella. Ornery." He squinted at me. "You'll understand that, I reckon."

I hated people having ideas about me. "What's it to anybody if I'm ornery?"

He squinted at me again. "What's your name?"

I didn't want anybody to know my name either. "Jim," I said.

"Well, Jim, I reckon you must have had a blame good reason for running off up here." He went on squinting at me.

"It ain't nobody's business," I said. "I got as much right up here as anybody."

He didn't say nothing for a minute. Then he said, "Look here, Jim, if that's your name, which I don't believe for a minute it is, it ain't easy for a grown man to get along up here, much less a kid. How much wood you got cut for the winter?"

I didn't say nothing. Then I said, "I ain't got no axe. How could I cut wood?"

"It don't matter what your excuse is. You get one heavy snow where you can't get outta your cabin, much less find wood, and the temperature's down below zero, you'll freeze to death overnight. Freeze solid as a rock. I seen it—fella was gray as lead and there was frost all around his mouth and nose from his last breaths. You better think about going home unless you got a damn good reason not to."

"I got a damn good reason." I was thinking about Ma. I was seven years old then. I got up one morning and there was Pa bent over the stove, stirring the oatmeal. "Where's Ma?" I said. "She sick?"

"She ain't here," Pa said.

"Where's she gone?"

"Don't know," Pa said. "She's just gone."

It was winter, cold as cold could be outside, the sky gray and coming up for snow, the men going by on the boardwalk in front of the store bundled up in sheepskins, clapping their hands to stay warm, and breathing out steam as thick as smoke. I couldn't understand what Pa was telling me. How could Ma disappear like that? "She can't be just gone. She must of went somewhere."

"She's just gone, Jesse." He took the oatmeal pan off the stove and put it on the kitchen table. "Now you eat your breakfast. You got to get to school. I ain't got all day. I got to get the store open." The store was down-stairs—we lived up over it.

It was all so strange. I couldn't believe what was happening. I began to lose hold of myself. "Pa, where's Ma?" I shouted. "I want Ma."

He grabbed me by the shoulder. "Jesse, get a hold of yourself. There ain't nothing I can do about it. She's gone. You got to get used to it. Now sit down and eat your breakfast."

I began to cry, my face all screwed up, the tears rolling down my cheeks.

"You stop that crying or I'll wallop you one. Hear me, Jesse?"

I couldn't stop. "Where'd she go, Pa? Where'd she go?"

"I told you I don't know. Now you stop that cater-wauling right this minute or you'll get a wallop."

"I can't stop, Pa." I clenched my mouth and eyes shut and shook my head, but no matter what I went on sobbing with the tears rolling down my cheeks and off my chin. He whacked me on the side of my head. "I told you to cut out that caterwauling, Jesse. Now eat your breakfast."

I wiped my face off with my sleeve and sat down in front of my bowl. But I couldn't eat nothing. I just sat there staring at the steam rising off the oatmeal, thinking, she'll come back. She has to come back. I know she will.

Pa stood there looking at me. Then he put his hand on my shoulder. "I'm sorry I walloped you, Jesse. I feel mighty bad myself. Try to eat something."

I looked at him. Somehow it made me feel better that

he felt bad about it, too. We was in the same boat. "Ain't she never coming back?"

"I got no doubts," he said. And she never did.

But none of that was good reason for being ornery with the mountain man. "What's your name?" I said. "I told you mine."

"What sorta name you want? How'd Frank do? Or Henry? Henry's a real nice name. Always liked it."

I went red—I seemed to do that a lot with him. "How come you're so certain my name ain't Jim?"

"Because it ain't."

Why was I being ornery with him? Here he caught me opening his traps, and instead of giving me a good beating, turned around and fed me dinner. What was the harm if he knew my name? I just had a feeling against it, was all—didn't want nobody to know nothing about me. "You still didn't tell me your name."

"Well I oughtn't to. But I ain't as techy as you. My name's Larry. And I'll tell you what—Jim. I believe you ought to do some serious thinking about this here problem you think you got at home. A lot of times they ain't near as bad as they seem at first."

"This one's bad."

"Well, I know it seems like it to you now. But mebbe back home they miss you and're ready to forget about it."

I didn't like him getting hisself mixed up in my troubles. I didn't like him getting in on my private business. He didn't know what it was all about. I stood up. "I got to thank you for dinner. It was blame tasty."

He looked at me for a minute. Then he stood up, too. "Okay, if that's the way you want it. But I'll make a deal with you. Next time you're hungry enough to eat a fox, come to me instead of fooling with my traps. I can always spare a little something."

"I won't touch your traps again."

"If you're that hungry, come and see me."

"I tell you what you can do," I said. "You can lend your axe for a couple of days so I can get up some wood."

He nodded. "I don't mind, so long as you put the edge back on it."

"Don't worry. Pa learned me how to sharpen an axe. I always did the ones in the store." The words was hardly out of my mouth when I tried to take them back. But it was too late. He didn't say anything, but pulled the axe out of the chopping block and handed it to me. I took it and went back to my lean-to.

Chapter Three

It was getting toward dusk when I got home. I found a rabbit in one of my snares, took it home and cleaned it, got a fire going, and stuck it on my spit to roast. I'd dug a pair of antlers I found in the woods into the ground so's the point stuck up, and laid the femur across the antlers. Made a pretty good spit, and I was proud of it—or *was* proud of it, before I seen the mountain man's set-up. And while the rabbit was cooking, I set there with my back against a tree, thinking.

That mountain man, he'd given me a lot of things to think about. I been up there in the mountains two, three weeks now—kind of lost track of the days. So far I managed to get along fair. I knew how to rig snares for small game, for me and Charlie Williams done it lots of times, trying to catch squirrels for their pelts. Squirrel skins wasn't worth much, but they was worth something and from time to time we got one. Charlie's pa knew how to cure them and when we got a half dozen or so we'd walk over to the trading post and swap 'em for a Barlow knife, a compass, some such thing that seemed mighty big to a seven-, eight-year-old kid.

So I knew all about catching small game and cleaning it, and I managed to get along on squirrels, rabbits, sometimes a pheasant or woodcock that got tangled in the snare. The wild strawberries was coming in, being as it was June. In July there'd be blueberries, and in August blackberries and such. There was a mountain lake I spotted around the mountain to the south—more a pond than a lake, half mile across maybe, but deep and bound to have fish in it. And twice I got deer.

Pa gave me a little gun for my tenth birthday. Oh, it was the best thing—just set me to glowing when he handed it over and said it was mine. For the first few days I didn't even shoot it, just laid it where I could look at it, and stared, feeling that glow. But then Pa said, "Jesse, that gun ain't no picture to hang on the wall, better learn how to shoot it." So I practiced up, and from time to time me and one or two of the kids I knew from school would go out onto the prairie hoping we'd come across a buffalo, but generally coming home with a couple of quail or a prairie dog, and mighty lucky to of got that. When I run off that day, the only thing I took was that gun, and my bag of powder and shot. So I could shoot and did some hunting when I come up there.

I searched around until I found deer trails. Climbed up into an oak over the trail, which had a nice broad branch I could dangle my legs down each side and set there, holding still as I could for hours at a stretch. I got lucky twice. A deer'd hold me for a few days.

But after talking to the mountain man, I could see I got to do better. Oh, I knew when I come up there I got to have a cabin—couldn't get through winter in no lean-to. But I was always too busy to get to it, and figured I had time enough, anyway.

Now I see I had a lot of things to worry about than just making a cabin. For one, that wall of wood the mountain man had stacked up alongside of his cabin wasn't there just so everybody could see how neat and tidy he got it. You wasn't going out in a howling blizzard to cut wood, for certain. You blame well better have enough to hand to get through a couple of weeks.

You wasn't going to hunt nothing in a howling blizzard neither. I got to have some meat salted down, or cured, or dried or something. And I got to have a fifty-pound sack of flour for biscuits and such, a slab of bacon, barrel of spuds, something, anything, so's I wouldn't starve when the bad weather come. For truck like that I needed money, and the only way to get money was to sell pelts. I been saving the pelts off the rabbits and squirrels I got, along with them two deer skins, but the truth is I didn't know how to cure them right, and they was beginning to stink. They prob'ly wasn't worth nothing anymore. I got to learn about them things, too. I could see now I hadn't of taken the whole business serious enough—just grabbed my gun and run off out of there. Of course I didn't have a whole lot of choice about it, after going for Pa with that axe handle. I wished I hadn't of done it. I wished I wouldn't lose hold of myself that way and fly off the handle. Seemed like I always been that way—just broke loose every once in a while and started flinging stuff around. Of course it was one thing to toss my supper on the floor. It was another to go after somebody with an axe handle. Still, he shouldn't of said to me what he said. It couldn't be true. It just couldn't. I shuddered, and to stop thinking about it I poked a stick into the rabbit meat to see if it was done.

The thing was, I couldn't build a cabin without no tools—needed an axe, saw, hammer, nails—maybe get away without the nails if I pegged the logs together, but then I'd need an auger to drill holes for the pegs. I could use a lot of other stuff, too—fish hooks, some more shot and powder, pry bar for moving rocks—oh, all kinds of stuff. Whyn't I given it a little thought instead of just high-tailing it out of there? Whyn't I at least grabbed an axe, saw or something?

What if I slipped back down there one night and loaded up? I knew of a window that wouldn't lock. Knew where everything was, too, and could find anything I wanted in the dark. In and out of there in five minutes, out of town in fifteen, and back across the prairie and onto the mountain in a couple of hours.

What if Pa was dead? What if somebody else had taken over the store? Maybe they'd fix that window so it'd lock, moved stuff around in the store so's I'd trip first thing, knock down a bunch of tools with a clatter fit to raise the dead. They'd be on me in a minute.

Maybe Pa's spirit would be hovering around the store waiting for me to turn up. Pa always said there wasn't no such thing as haunts and spirits, there wasn't no God neither, nor Heaven nor Hell 'cept right here on earth, and a lot more Hell than Heaven so far as that went. I wasn't sure. Ma always seen that I got to church with her on Sunday. Pa wouldn't go. Said he had plenty enough to do without wasting a morning singing and praying. But Ma was all for it. I reckoned there was a God. Didn't seem to me any way there *couldn't* be one. Was He looking down on me, thinking to Hisself, what'm I going to do about that boy who kilt his own father? Maybe He hadn't noticed yet. It didn't seem likely that Pa was headed for Heaven, not when he said there wasn't no Heaven in the first place. If you didn't believe in it, how could you go there? So maybe God hadn't noticed Pa was dead yet. Maybe He didn't care one way or another even if He did notice. Anyways, He hadn't struck me dead so far, and I figured if He hadn't of yet, He wasn't likely to. Mark it down against me, maybe, but let it go at that.

Whatever God thought about it, it bothered me plenty, especially when I remembered swinging that axe handle around, felt that thump in my hands, and heard that loud click. Whenever it came to my mind I stopped dead whatever I was doing, began to breathe hard and fast. And I'd tell God I didn't mean it, I just lost hold of myself. But the truth was, right then I meant it. He shouldn't of said what he said.

If only Ma hadn't disappeared. Everything was all about that. For a long time there, I figured he killed her. Lost his temper the way he did sometimes and smacked her with something. Finally one day when we was fighting—can't even remember what over, but I went for him and was hammering at him with my fists, and I shouted out, "You

killed Ma, goddamn you, I'm going to kill you for it."
Eight, I was, maybe.

Well, he calmed right down. He grabbed a hold of
my hands, held them together between his hands, and
said in a soft way, "I never did, Jesse. Is that what you
been thinking all this while? I never did."

When he spoke to me in that soft way I stopped struggling and stared at him. He went on holding my hands.
"Is that what you been thinking? I never did. I loved
her, Jesse, as much as a man can love someone. She
didn't want to stay." I began to cry, and he pulled me to
him and hugged me for a while. "Poor baby," he said.
"Poor baby." After that I reckoned he didn't kill her. But
in a way that was worse, for it meant that she'd left
because she wanted to, not because she had to. I hated to
think about that, too.

I shook my head to get all such ideas off me. "Jesse," I
said out loud, "you got to stop dwelling on things all the
time. It don't do no good." I took the rabbit off the fire,
blew on it to cool it down, and when it was cool enough
I began to gnaw on it. When I was finished I flung the
bones in the fire and wiped my hands off on the dead
leaves and grass. Then I lay back, thinking and watching
the stars pop out one by one. It always surprised me that
they didn't ease out slowly—just a tiny speck and get
bigger and bigger. Instead, they just popped out—wasn't
there one minute, was there the next.

No way around it, I had to go down to the store and
see what I could find. No sense putting it off. It was

stealing, no way around it. I didn't like the idea of stealing very much. Stealing from your pa wasn't the same as stealing in general, I figured; it was all in the family. Still, it was stealing. Of course I worked in that store all my life since I was big enough to hold a broom. But I'd got my keep out of it, so that came out even. No matter how I wriggled around, I couldn't get out of it—it was stealing. But I didn't have no choice. The best I could do to make up for it was feel bad about it. I'd do that—for a couple of days, anyway.

I needed a cloudy night. I didn't want no moon, that was certain. In bright moonlight you could see somebody moving on the prairie for miles. The sun was shining in the morning, and I woke up determined to do better for myself. The first thing I done was to walk on up the mountain, looking for a real good spot for my cabin. I walked around all morning, and then when the sun was overhead, beaming down through the trees in wide streams, I found a place that struck me just right. The mountain here was just a rock wall. Below it the ground was level and grassy—one of them cleared spots you found. Lots of rocks scattered around, real handy to make a stone base for the cabin—you wanted the wood up off the ground so it wouldn't rot. Coming off the rock wall was a small stream from a spring a good way up the mountain. It splashed onto the rocks at the bottom of the wall, sparkling and flashing in the sun, then ran across the clearing and wound down through the forest as it sloped off. Stream from a spring like that'd run in the driest weather. It was a mighty pretty spot.

I set down on a rock to take it all in. Being as it was late in June the grass was up a good foot. A little breeze came down the mountain behind me, and ran across the prairie grass, bending it over. All of a sudden I was reminded of a hand brushing through cat's fur, and I knew that the memory was going to come, and the bad feeling with it. I felt the knots grow in my stomach, my muscles clench up, the skin of my head pull tight. I was back in that shed, all by myself alone, staring out across the hayfield to the woods below where something was happening that I hated. I jumped up and sucked in the biggest mouthful of air I could manage. Damn it all to hell, I thought, why did that feeling always come? Why couldn't I recall what I seen in these woods? My stomach was cramped up like somebody'd got a fist in there and was squeezing it. I took in another deep breath, straightened up, and began to walk in circles round and round; and by and by the cramps eased off and I was all right again.

No, I like this place, I'm going to stick it out here. I ain't gonna let that thing run me out of here. This is gonna be my place. It's gonna be mine.

I had sun the next day, too, so I spent it chopping wood. Done that since I was little, too—split all the kindling for us from the time I was seven. I couldn't keep the mountain man's axe for more'n a couple of days. He'd need it. So I banged away all day, determined to get a start on my wall of wood, even if I didn't have no cabin to stack it up against yet, and by the time the day was over I had a fair heap of wood laying up behind where I'd got the rock foundation to my cabin.

I couldn't keep the axe no longer—wasn't right. I had to take it back to the mountain man. The thing was, I was worried that he might think I wanted to be friendly. I didn't want him to get no idea like that. It didn't suit me. So I figured I'd go on up there in the morning when he was out checking his trapline, and leave it there for him. I went on over there. But just to be safe, I slipped through the woods up behind his cabin, and lay in the shadows spotted with sun, smelling the sharp sweet smell of the hemlock grove, and the musty smell of the oaks.

The mountain man was down there, stripped to the waist, washing out some clothes in that big turtle shell. Good sunny day for drying clothes. It made me feel uneasy, for I hadn't washed nothing at all for a while. I figured I must smell pretty bad, but what did it matter, for there wasn't nobody to smell me. Still, I figured I ought to try to keep myself clean.

How soon would he finish up and go off? I reckoned he didn't have no dresser full of clothes—couple of shirts, couple of pants, some socks. Wouldn't take that long to wash. I could wait. Besides, I kind of liked watching him down there. Couldn't figure out why that'd be so, but it was. Felt nice to watch him dipping them shirts into the turtle shell, rub 'em up with a chunk of yellow soap, wrestle them around for a while, twist 'em up tight like a rope to squeeze the water out, and hang 'em up to dry on anything handy—sawbuck, woodpile.

Then he finished. But instead of getting his gun and going off to the trapline, he went into the cabin. In a minute he came out with some knives and a stone, set down on the chopping block, and began working on the knife blades with the stone.

Well, I was stuck. I couldn't lay up there in the forest all day waiting for him to leave, and I couldn't keep the axe no longer—he needed it. I didn't have no choice. I told myself, I'll just go on down there, talk enough to be polite, leave the axe, and take myself off. Say I moved my snares and got to see how they was doing. So I stood up out of the shadows and walked on down. He seen me coming before I got ten feet—got in the habit of keeping his eyes and ears open from being in the mountains so long.

I come into the clearing. "I brung your axe back."

"So I see," he said. He stopped working the stone, and run his finger over the knife edge. "You get any use out of it?"

"Got a start on a stack of wood." I looked over at his long wall of wood. Just looking at it made me feel down. I got some job ahead of me to catch up to him. "How much you figure I'm gonna need?"

"Two, three cords," he said.

I wasn't sure how big a cord was, but I knew it was big. "That what you got there?"

"That's about two cords. Get me two more before the snow flies, I reckon."

"That's a blame lot of wood," I said. I knew I better get out of there before we got to be friendly with each other. What if he asked me to stay for some ham and biscuits?

36

"You'd do a blame sight better with a saw," he said. "Make yourself a sawbuck like that one I got. Good sharp saw'll slice through a log like butter."

"I ain't got no nails for starts," I said.

"Well, I wouldn't mind lending you a few."

That was what I been afraid of. I better get out of there. "That's mighty kind, but I guess I can manage." I held out the axe. "Here's your axe. Thanks."

He didn't take the axe, but squinted at me. "I don't suppose if I asked you to set a spell you'd take an interest in it. I was thinking it might be time for something to eat."

"That's mighty kind, but I set out a new snare yesterday and I better check it."

He shrugged, and picked up another knife. He didn't say nothing.

"I better go," I said.

"I ain't stopping you," he said.

I leaned the axe against the block with the turtle shell on it. "Well, so long."

"So long, Jim," he said. "Drop by anytime."

I turned and went, feeling rotten and sore at myself. Whyn't I set for a while? Why'd I always have to be so ornery?

Chapter Four

Two days later I got my clouds. They began scudding in during the afternoon, and by supper time they was mighty thick. Looked like rain all right. I didn't fancy the idea of parading all the way into town in the rain, but I didn't have no choice. I needed clouds, and rain was likely to come with them.

I set off when night was coming, but there was still some gray light coming down through the trees, so's I could get off that mountain before it got too dark. Once I was on the prairie I'd be able to see the glow from the town and follow it in. There wasn't no real road from the mountains into town, but over the years hunters and such had worn a track into the prairie. I'd be all right once I got onto the prairie.

So I went on down through the gray shadowy woods, hoping that Pa was still alive and his spirit wouldn't be hovering up by the ceiling of the store. And what if he was still alive, like I figured, and come downstairs and caught me? He'd wham the tar out of me, that was certain. Had a right to beat me half to death, I figured. Didn't reckon he'd kill me. Come close, though.

It took me a couple of hours to get down off the mountain, working my way through the trees in the gray light. But then I was on the prairie. Ahead of me was a faint yellowy light—not much to it, but enough so's I knew where the town was. I wasn't in no rush now. I figured it was around eight, and I wouldn't want to climb through the window into the store until the town settled in for the night. So I took my time going in, stumbling along the track, hoping that I didn't step on no rattlesnake. By and by the yellowy glow began to separate out into spots of light, where people hadn't gone to bed yet, and lamps was shining through their windows.

Oh, I knew that little town like the back of my hand. Didn't know everybody there, for in a place like that people was always coming and going. Turn up there looking for work, looking to buy a farm out in the country somewhere around, looking to trade with the Indians, looking to start some little business. Then they'd go—farther West, maybe, up to Oregon, out to California. Or get tired of empty prairie and the life out there and go back home. They came and went.

But a lot of them stayed, and I knew them—knew where they lived, knew their stories, knew who got born in this house, who died in that one, like Charlie Williams. To be honest, there wasn't much to it—maybe a hundred houses rowed up along two streets running this way, and three more running across them. Two churches, three saloons, our store, a little bank, a feed store with the post office in it. That was it.

I stood there for a minute, feeling kind of strange. I'd been part of that little town all my life—knew everybody and everything, for everybody in town had to come into the store from time to time and the gossip just flew there. It was home to me, that little town—only home I ever knew. Everything just as familiar as could be.

But I'd moved myself outside of it. It was like when you get up to being ten, eleven years old, and go back to where you used to play hoops and such when you was six or seven, trying to see who could roll your hoop the longest, and there are some six- or seven-year-old kids playing there just like you done. And you join in with them, but it isn't the same, for you outgrowed it. It don't matter like it used to. That's the way I felt standing there on the outskirts of that little town—familiar and all, but I wasn't really part of it no more.

I shook the feeling off—wouldn't do no good to have a lot of feelings like that, when I had so much to do. I set off around the back of town, keeping well away from the lights falling out of some of the windows. It was plenty dark, but I knew where all the houses was, where their sheds was, and who had clotheslines running from the shed to the house and such. A couple of times I started dogs barking, but I knew who they were and they knew who I was and I shushed 'em down pretty quick.

Finally I come down the alley that run behind the store. I hunkered down alongside the corner of the shed where Pa stored stuff—bolts of cloth, barrels of molasses, boxes of lamp mantles. I looked up. There wasn't no lights on in the store, but there was a light on in Pa's bedroom upstairs. If it still was Pa's. Was some stranger living up there now? I kind of shuddered. Come to think of it, if Pa was dead maybe the place was mine now. Although I reckoned maybe you couldn't make a claim on a place if you killed the owner.

I waited, hunkered down in the dark, and after a bit the light upstairs went out. I stood up and went on waiting. Pa was a light sleeper, tossed and turned and was likely to get up in the middle of the night to get hisself a glass of water. Time dragged on slow as a funeral song. I counted off the seconds. I was feeling pretty nerved up by now, and when a dog barked in the distance I jumped. Fidgety and itchy all over. I told myself, in a half hour, fifteen minutes maybe, it'd be all over. Just hang on a little.

So I done that. Finally I couldn't stand it no more. I slipped away from the shed, crossed the backyard, and went on around to the side of the store where the unlocked window was. For a minute I knelt there by the window, listening. No sounds from inside. Nothing.

Was the window still unlocked? I put my hands on the sash and pushed upward. The window eased open an inch. Unlocked. Took a deep breath and eased it up a little. It gave off a sudden squeal and I come near to letting it drop. I knelt there, dead still, my heart thumping like a dog's tail on a wood floor. Blame it. How come I never noticed that window squeal before? Probably done it for years and I never noticed. Why hadn't I put a little bacon grease on it?

It was too late for bacon grease. I inched the window up a little more. There wasn't no squeal, so I pushed it up and here come that squeal again like a puppy got stepped on. I stood still and listened. Nothing: no sound from upstairs. I give it another minute, trying to breathe real quiet. Still nothing. I propped the window open with the stick that was right there where it always was, and slid over the window sill into the store.

For a minute I crouched by the window, listening again. All the old familiar smells come wafting into my nose—smell of gun oil, tarry smell of rope, smell of new cloth from the blue shirts and overalls stacked on the shelves against the near wall, smell of leather sacks and belts. I smelled those smells all my life and never given them a thought before. Now they come rolling over me, carrying all them memories with them: Ma with her hair done up behind her head sitting at the counter doing the accounts—she was a better hand at it than Pa; Pa crouched by a molasses barrel that had sprung a leak, cussing it out like it was a horse; Ma coming downstairs on a spring Sunday morning in her nightgown, barefoot, her hair long behind, to get some sugar for coffee. Oh, I spent the whole of my life in that store among them smells. Crouching there under the window it took hold of my heart and I wished I was back there in them days and Ma was still coming downstairs barefoot with her hair down behind to fill up the yellow sugar bowl.

And who was sleeping upstairs? Was it Pa in his old blue nightcap and blue-striped nightgown Ma made for him, all patched up now, his face a little stubby from not having shaved for a couple of days. Or was it some stranger I never seen before?

I shook myself. Jesse, mustn't have them thoughts. I raised myself up, kicked off my shoes, and eased barefoot across the store, to where the tools was ranged up along the far wall, holding my hand out in front of me just in case things wasn't in their same place anymore. Then I felt along the wall, moving my hand slow and easy, until I hit something. I ran my hand over it: axe. Keeping one hand on it, I felt around some more until I got hold of a shovel. I slipped back across the floor, my heart thumping away like a drum, and eased the shovel and axe out the window. Then I crossed the floor again, and fumbled around until I found a saw, a pick, and a hank of rope. I slipped back to the window and eased them out, too. I would have liked to take a pry bar for moving rocks around, but it was too much to carry, so I stuck a hammer and an awl in my belt, and filled up my pockets with ten-penny nails. I headed back for the window once more, just as eager to get out of there as could be. Blame if them nails didn't give a good chink every step I took. I grabbed hold of the pockets from the outside to hold them still, but there was still some loose that went on chinking. I got to the window, and then there come a noise from upstairs—feet hitting the floor with a thump.

For a little bit there was quiet, and then out the window I saw a glow. He'd lit a lamp. Blame them jingling nails.

I was out the window quick as a cat. I slipped the coil of rope over my shoulders, and tied the saw handle to the slack end. Then I snatched up the axe and the shovel with one hand, the pick with the other and began to slip away, dodging around the patch of light falling down from the bedroom window, running on my tiptoes as best as I could with that load.

I reached the alley and turned to look back. The light in the windows was bouncing the shadows around—he was carrying the lantern down the stairs. As soon as he saw the open window he'd known some robber had just climbed through it, and he'd set up a whoop and cry. I told myself, never mind about tiptoeing, and began to run for the prairie. They wouldn't dare come after me on horseback at night, for fear of the horse stepping in a hole and busting a leg, and like as not busting the rider, too.

I went on running. Them nails was jingling away like a brass band, and the axe head was clanging on the shovel like a bell. I sounded like a junk wagon going by. On I ran until I was clear of town. I stopped and turned to look back.

There wasn't nothing going on—nothing to see but a few points of light where people was still up—couldn't sleep, drinking and playing cards, rocking a baby that had the colic. No shouting; all quiet. He'd given up—figured the robber had got away.

I shifted my load around so's things wouldn't jingle so much, and settled into a steady walk, just putting one foot in front of the other, stumbling from time to time, for now the light was behind me and there wasn't nothing ahead but dark. But I wasn't going to have no trouble finding the mountain—I was bound to bump into it sooner or later. And a couple of hours later I did. I felt my way up in there until I was pretty well hid in the trees and lay down to wait for first light.

As soon as I closed my eyes the first raindrops hit. Nothing to do about it. I sat up and huddled myself together. The rain got heavy until it was pouring down steady. I was soaked through pretty quick. Oh, that night seemed to go on just forever, the minutes dragging along like they was on crutches. Finally the color of the dark changed a little. I waited, and in half an hour I could see enough to make my way back up to my lean-to. I got in out of the rain, stripped down, covered myself over with one of my deerskins, bad as it smelt, and feeling lonely and sad as the last person on earth, I fell asleep, and slept until noon.

By the middle of the afternoon it stopped raining and started to blow off. I got a fire going and dried out my clothes—they needed a wash anyway. Then I went on up to my new territory with the shovel, axe, and saw, determined to get going on my cabin. It'd cheer me up to do something. I marked out the ground with a stick a square eight feet by eight. Mighty small cabin, but I wanted to get something up as soon as I could so I could turn my attention to building a wall of firewood. It'd do for a start. I trenched along the stick mark and set rocks in the trench for my foundation. Then I started to work on my logs. First saw down a tree about eight inches through, trim off the branches, saw it into eight-foot lengths. Then I'd notch the ends so's I could fit one log over the other. I wished I could have used bigger logs, say a foot through, for with bigger logs I needed only six or so to a side. But I couldn't handle a log that big— hard enough to handle the smaller ones.

So I started laying up the logs. Of course, they never fit just right; I had to keep trying them, then pulling them off and working the notch a little more, or taking out bulges, until I got them real snug. It took me a good hour to do each log—slow going. Oh, it was hard work, and boring, but I seen that if I kept on plugging away I'd get her done. Slow as it went, it cheered me up a good deal, for I could see that I *would* have myself a snug cabin before the snow come.

I needed the cheering up, for after five, six days of working on the cabin, along with catching enough food to keep up my strength, and never seeing another person the whole time, the loneliness was hitting me pretty good. It wasn't so bad when I was working—notching out logs, setting out my snares and such. But when I wasn't doing nothing it hit me pretty fierce—a kind of deep misery that took all the stuffings out of me. Mighty bothersome at night, especially, when I set by my fire with nobody to talk to, waiting until I was tired enough to sleep. A couple of times I went over to the rock outcropping, hoping I'd see some people out on the prairie —train of overlanders with high hopes for Oregon or wherever they was going, two or three pals riding home from hunting buffalo. But I didn't see nobody.

I cursed myself for the loneliness—it was a weakness. I come up into the mountains of my own free will, bound and determined to live by myself. And here come all this loneliness. It was a weakness, all right. Finally I saw I couldn't go on this way. I just had to set and talk with somebody for a while. So I give myself a little wash-up in the stream, and went around the corner of the mountain to see if Larry wasn't at home.

He wasn't; but just being near signs of a human being was a help—his old coat hanging on a wall peg, tin dishes on the table, half-chewed biscuit on the chopping block. I reckoned to wait for him, and to pass the time I studied out the way he put his cabin together, to see if there was some stunts I ought to know about it.

He'd sawed a window through the logs in each side of the cabin, framed up the holes, and covered them over with oil paper that he could roll up when the weather was good. Light'd come through paper if you oiled it. I could frame up windows like that and cover them with skins in bad weather, until I got hold of some paper. If I ever figured out how to cure skins right.

But his chimney was a mystery. I looked it over. It

seemed to be plastered up with something, but there was twigs inside the plaster stuff, for I could see ends poking out here and there. What'd he made the plaster out of? And I was about to go inside to stick my head up the chimney when he come into the clearing carrying a small four-point buck over his shoulder. Just seeing him cheered me up a good deal.

"Well," he said. "From the way you was talking here the other day I reckoned I wouldn't see you for a month of Sundays."

"Oh, I was just going by and thought I might as well stop in and see how you was doing."

"Oh, was you?" He flung the buck off his shoulder and onto the ground, knelt beside, and skinned it out as quick as lightning, zip-zip, slash-slash there was the skin off neat as could be.

I hoped he'd set about curing it so's I could learn how he done it. "I guess you had a lot of practice skinning game."

"I guess I have," he said. He looked up at me from where he was quartering the buck. "Hungry?"

I was, but I wasn't going to ask for no favors. "No thanks. I got me a rabbit in a snare this morning."

"That won't hold you for long."

"I'm not hungry."

"Still mighty techy, ain't you? Got lonely I expect."

I blushed for being caught out, and turned my head so he wouldn't notice. "It don't bother me none to be alone.

I like it. But it makes a change to talk to somebody."

He gave me a look. "I reckon it does." He went back to quartering the deer.

"The littlest I see of people the better I like it."

He gave me another look. The buck's guts were laying on the ground. He picked them up and cut the liver loose, his hands all bloody. "I reckon I go along with you there. I like my own company pretty well. But you got to talk to somebody now and again. Don't do to keep to yourself too long. Get to seeing things if you do. It happened to me once. I got way up in the mountains, down to the south end of the Big Horn somewheres, and got myself all twisted around. Was up there near two weeks before I figured out where I was. The last couple of days I kept seeing Indians popping out of everywhere—behind trees, bushes, rocks. At first I thought they was real and would holler at them for help. But then I seen one of them step off a cliff and walk down through the air, like they was stairs there. I knew I was seeing things. I reckoned if I'd of stayed up there a couple more days I'd been crazy as a hoot owl."

I thought: if Larry could get lonely like that, maybe it wasn't such a weakness when I done it, too. Maybe he was right—a fella had to talk to somebody now and again. "How'd you get out?"

"Round about then I heard a gunshot. Thought I was hearing things, too, but then I saw some crows fly up over the forest and I figured it was real. I tracked after the gunshot, and come across a fella who knew where he was. So glad to see a human being, Jesse, I come near to falling on my knees and kissing his shoes."

I stared at him. "How'd you know my name was Jesse? I told you it was Jim."

He looked at me again. "Did I say Jesse? I must of made a mistake. I was thinking of another Jesse I know."

He'd been talking to somebody about me, that was plain. I didn't like being rumpled over by people. "You didn't make no mistake. You been talking to somebody."

"Well, as a matter of fact, I have."

"Who?" I said. "You have to tell me."

"I don't have to tell you nothing if I don't want. But I will. It was your pa."

Chapter Five

"**P**a?" I stood there trying to catch a hold of my feelings. Even though I hated the idea of him and Pa talking about me, I was mighty relieved. "Pa's all right?"

"He's got a pretty good scar behind his ear. But he said you didn't mess up his brains no more than they was already."

"He ain't sore at me?"

"Didn't seem like it. He said he wished you'd get some sense in your head and come home. He said he figured when winter come and you was freezing your tail off, you'd change your mind about it."

"He really ain't sore at me?"

"I don't reckon he'd encourage you to do it again, but he don't seem sore. Worried, more like it."

I stood there staring down at the ground and frowning. It was the blamedest thing: I couldn't figure out whether I was glad or sorry about it. Mighty glad that I didn't bust him up anymore than I did, that was certain; but felt kind of strange that he wasn't sore at me. It didn't fit. He *ought* to be sore at me. That was the point right there: he ought to be sore at me. "Well, it surprises me some that he ain't sore at me."

I looked up and seen that he had been staring at me the whole time. "Don't surprise me none," he said. "I reckon it's what any pa would do." He looked down at the deer guts. "Although I reckon I oughtn't to speak. I never been a pa, and never had one myself."

"You never had a pa? He die or something?"

He didn't say anything for a minute. "It don't do no good to dwell on it," he said finally.

But I was thinking what it must have been. "I'll bet he run off on you."

He stood up. "You gonna eat some of this here deer meat or are you too techy for that?"

So we was in the same boat, him and me. Was that why he was always wanting to help me out here and there? "Did you know my ma run off on me?"

He stopped and looked off into the woods. "Yes, I knew that, once I figured out who you was."

"How'd you know?"

"Jesse, for God's sake, everyone in town knew about it. It was all the talk when it happened."

"Oh," I said. "I guess I should of realized that. I never give it any thought."

"In a little town like that, where the most exciting thing ever happened was some cowboy got drunk and shot hisself in the foot, they wasn't about to pass up gossip like that."

"I guess so," I said. "I reckon nobody knew why she done it, though, or where she went."

"No, nobody knew that."

"It wasn't on account of me, though."

He gave me a funny look. "Who said it was?"

It had been Pa, which was why I took a swing at him with the axe handle. But I wasn't going to tell Larry nothing about it. "Nobody. I just thought somebody might of."

"Not that I heard of," Larry said. "Life is hard enough as it is without inventing troubles for yourself, Jesse. I wonder why you'd want to think your ma run off on account of you."

"Didn't want to think it, because it ain't true." I changed the subject. "I got me a start on my cabin." Then I realized I was giving something away. "I got hole of a saw and an axe."

"So I heard."

I blushed. "How'd Pa know it was me?"

"He said couldn't of nobody else found their way around the store in the pitch dark without making a clatter fit to raise the dead."

"Oh," I said. "Well, I had to get some tools, didn't I?"

"I ain't blaming you, am I? You gonna make that fire or ain't you?"

I took a deep breath. I knew I ought to go. I knew I oughn't to get myself lured in. But there was so many things swirling around in my brain I couldn't think straight about it. "I reckon so," I said.

So I scared up some wood and got a fire going, and then we hunkered down there while he fried up a nice chunk of meat, and we chitchatted. "What I can't figure is how you was talking to Pa about me in the first place."

"Well, it come up because this here fella Billings I told you about was in there talking to your pa about you. Wanted to know if he heard anything from you. Your pa, he looked mournful and said he hadn't heard nothing, but he figured you was in the mountains, and would come back when your tail started to freeze."

"What was Billings asking that for? You said he knew I was up here and didn't like it none."

"Well, yes, that struck me, too. Seemed like he didn't want to let on he knew you was up here." Larry sat there frowning and thinking about something. Finally he said, "Well, it ain't none of my business to tell you this, but I reckon I better, just so's you know. The story I heard was that Billings got run out of California for something he done over there. Was working a placer mine, looking for gold like the rest of them idiots, and got hisself in trouble, and they run him out of there."

"What kind of trouble?"

"Story I heard was, he killed some fella. Had a grievance against him, caught him alone in the woods somewhere and cut his throat. Cold-blooded. Planned it out." He sat there thinking some more. "Now that's the story I heard, Jesse. I ain't saying it's the gospel truth. No shortage of killings around them gold fields. Wouldn't surprise me none if it was true, wouldn't surprise me none if it was all just a story. Only thing is, might be a good idea if you stayed clear of him."

The whole thing worried me a good deal. "I still don't get why he wouldn't tell Pa he knew I was up here."

"Like I say, it struck me that way, too. Wasn't none of my business, but your pa, he looked so mournful I figured I'd let him know you was alive. So I said I heard there was a boy running wild in the mountains scaring off game."

I didn't like the idea that they was talking about me neither. "What'd this Billings say then?"

"He had to backtrack pretty quick. 'Oh, that boy,' he said. 'Maybe that's your Jesse. Wonder why I didn't think of it before.' Some such."

"What'd you say then?"

"Nothing. Just let it drop. Wasn't none of my business what he told your pa."

"Oh," I said. The whole thing was bothering me a lot. Didn't like this Billings taking an interest in me, that was certain. Didn't like any of 'em talking about me in the first place. Why couldn't nobody just leave me alone? "You didn't tell Pa where I was living or nothing?"

"No. It wasn't none of my business to do that. But I figured there wasn't no harm in it if he knew you was alive and hadn't got et by a mountain jack."

I was thankful for that. But I couldn't bring myself to say so. The closest I could come was, "I just as soon he wasn't looking for me up here to whale the tar out of me."

"Jesse, I don't think that's what he had in mind. Give you a hug and kiss, more like."

"Not Pa. He ain't big on hugs and kisses."

"Well, maybe not. I don't reckon he's of a mind to whale you neither." He poked at the deer meat with a knife. "He must of said something real bad to get you so riled up you went after him with an axe handle."

"He did," I said. I didn't want to talk about it. "We wasn't getting along too good around that time, anyway. I guess I was reaching the age where in general I didn't want nobody telling me what to do."

What Pa said was, "Jesse, if your ma seen the way you been behaving in recent weeks it'd of broke her heart." It was the first he mentioned her in a while—he didn't never talk about her much. It kind of took me back, and I said, "She didn't run off on account of me." And he said back right quick, "Don't think you didn't have nothing to do with it, Jesse." That's when I lost ahold of myself. I snatched up an axe handle from where they was laying on a shelf and swung at him. I wasn't aiming at any particular place on him, just sore and swinging. He was turning away, bent a little. He didn't see it coming and it caught him behind the ear. I didn't say any of this to Larry, though. All I said was, "Pa said something that took me wrong."

He jabbed at the meat again. "This here meat's done," he said. "Let's eat."

I could see there was subjects he didn't want to talk about. Like to keep his mouth shut about most things. So there was things I was going to have to figure out for myself, and the next day, when I was banging at those logs I was busy thinking.

What difference did it make to Pa if I come back to the store? Oh, I was a good worker, and knew how things was supposed to be in the store, but on the other hand he had to feed me and clothe me and give me a few cents from time to time for hard candy and such. Besides, I went to school now and again, especially in the winter when things was slow. I wasn't any use to him when I was in school, unless he figured I needed to know how to do sums and write good if I was to take care of the store for him some day. But otherwise, why'd he want me back? I wasn't no bargain when I lost hold of myself and went rampaging around tossing stuff all over the place. Once I scaled all our tin plates out the kitchen window. They flew a good way, shining in the sun, and landed in the Widow Wadman's yard that lived next door to us and scared her cow such that she gave sour milk for a week. Another time I went through the store and knocked all the shirts and pants onto the floor and stomped on them. Tried to rip them up, too, but they was too strong for me. Another time I took a case of lantern chimneys, thin glass, and smashed them one at a time in the street in front of the house. Oh, he couldn't do nothing with me when I lost hold of myself. Of course he made me wash out all them shirts and pants and put them back, and hoe Widow Wadman's turnips for a week to show I was sorry. Still, I wasn't no bargain. Why'd he want me back there with him? Glad to be shet of me I'd of thought. Good riddance.

But he told Larry he wanted me back with him, and knowing Pa, he wasn't likely to rest until he done it. Would he come up here looking for me? I wouldn't of put it past him. It was just what he'd do. I'd have to keep my eyes open.

Then, that fella Billings needed some thinking about, too. Why'd he want to keep it from Pa that he knew I was up there in the mountains? Larry, he told Pa right away I was alive, so's to make Pa feel better. Whyn't Billings do the same? Why'd he want Pa to think he didn't know nothing about me, when he already told Larry he wanted me out of the mountains? I couldn't see no reason for it. Billings, he was up to something. But I couldn't figure what.

For the next couple of weeks I went along whacking away at my new cabin until I'd got the walls up—about six and a half feet on the front, four and a half on the back, so the roof would have a good pitch. You wanted it to slant so's the snow would slide off, for if it build up too heavy the weight would bust the roof in.

Once I got the logs up, I chinked in between them with moss, pieces of bark and such, to make the walls wind- and watertight. The chinking wouldn't last forever —I'd have to repair leaks now and again, but it'd last for a while.

Next I cut a door in the front about five feet high, and framed it up with some boards I cut out of some of the logs I had left. I was glad I'd taken the awl out of the store, for instead of wasting nails I could drill holes in the framing boards and peg them to logs with pegs I carved out of green branches. I got the door hole done in a day. It was a neat job and I was mighty proud of myself, and stood looking at it for a while when I got it done. Before winter come, I'd hang skins down in front of it to keep the wind and snow out.

Then I set about making my roof. More logs to cut and notch, but I'd got to where I was pretty swift with them notches now, and it didn't take me but four days to get them roof logs laid up and snugged together nice and tight. Still, she'd leak when it rained. I had enough sense to know that you couldn't chink up a roof with no moss. Chinking like that was all right on a wall, where the water'd run off. On a roof the water wouldn't run off, but would pool there in holes and pockets. Soon enough it would soak in, and drip through.

How'd you chink a roof? I was blamed if I knew. Larry's cabin was dry enough. I decided I better have a look at it and see how he done his roof. Besides, to tell the truth, that loneliness was coming on me again. I hated giving into that loneliness—didn't like to feel I couldn't get along without people. But that loneliness was powerful strong. Too strong for me, I had to admit. So I went around the mountain to Larry's place.

I was getting to know my part of the mountain pretty good. Been all over it for two, three miles around looking for animal trails, setting snares, tracking deer. I knew where all the springs was, knew where the different kind of berries grew, knew where there was a blow-down, the logs lying across each other every which way so's you could hardly get through, knew where there was an easy way through the trees. It was getting to be home to me, and I liked the feeling of it—liked knowing what I was doing up there, where a lot of folks wouldn't. I had a right to feel proud, I reckoned. It wasn't no soft life up there.

Larry wasn't home. That kind of disappointed me. Still, it was a help just to be where some other human lived. I went inside and took a look at his ceiling. It was chinked in with the same stuff he'd made the chimney out of. It was hard, but still, it'd soften up where water pooled and had a chance to soak in.

I went outside, rolled his chopping block over to the side of the cabin, climbed up, and had a look at the roof. There was the answer: he'd covered the roof logs with sheets of bark and pinned them down with big flat rocks. Bark was watertight—had to be to keep the tree inside from drowning. I knew where I could get all the bark I wanted. There was a lot of hemlocks down in one of them blow-downs. They was starting to rot, and the bark was hanging off them in big sheets. I had plenty of rocks up by my cabin that'd tumbled down the rock wall. Fixing my roof would be easy as pie, now I seen how it was done. I should of thought it myself.

That only left the chimney. I climbed down off the chopping block, rolled it back to where it belonged, and went back to the chimney to have a look at it real close.

And I was in the midst of this when Larry come home, carrying a fox hide he'd skinned out in the woods. He give me a look. "I could tell you where to find that there clay, but you'd think I was doing you a favor and get techy about it."

"I expect I would," I said, wishing I wasn't saying it. "I get techy real easy."

"I noticed," he said.

There went my chance; but at least now I knew it was clay from somewheres near around. Maybe I could find it. "I see you got yourself a fox."

"Yep. I seen bear tracks out there, too. He was sniffing around my traps. I must of scared him off when he smelt me coming up. He headed on up the mountain looking for berries, I reckon. A good bear skin's worth a lot of money."

That sparked my interest all right. There was a whole lot of things I wanted money for—sack of flour, big flitch of bacon, powder, balls. You couldn't get along in them mountains without some money.

But taking on a bear was pretty scary. They said you could shoot a bear in the heart and it'd keep on coming. Did I have the guts to take on a bear? Of course it wasn't my bear, anyway, it was Larry's. "You going after it?"

"I reckon I'll have a look. He's got to be up there somewhere." He gave me a glance. "You reckon you want to go up there with me?"

There wasn't nothing I wanted more. Not for just the money that might come out of it neither; it would be an adventure. How many fellas ever hunted a bear? But I didn't want him doing me no favors neither. "You seen him first. I reckon he's your bear."

"I ain't seen nothing but a couple of prints yet."

"Even so," I said, praying that he'd argue with me.

He shrugged. "Have it your own way," he said. I wished he would of argued with me. Blame it all, why didn't I say yes right off? Then suddenly I saw he was disappointed. That sure surprised me. Why'd he feel disappointed about it? He'd of had to share the money with me if I'd of went with him.

"I seen your pa again," he said.

"You did? What'd he say about me?"

"He wanted to know if I seen you. I told him you'd been around. He said was you all right? I said so far as I could judge you was."

"Did he say he was coming up here after me?"

Larry nodded. "Yes. He did say that."

"Did you tell him where my cabin was?"

"No. It wasn't none of my business to do that. Far as that goes, I ain't seen your cabin myself."

"Do you think Billings knows where my cabin is?" I said.

"I got an idea Billings is keeping a pretty good eye on you. But I don't reckon he's told your pa where your cabin's at, for your pa would of come up here to see you by now."

The whole thing worried me a good deal. "How come Billings being so closed mouth about me with Pa?"

He shrugged. "Don't reckon I could say for sure. Seems likely he don't want anyone to know he's taken an interest in you."

"But you think he knows where my cabin's at?"

"He'll find it. You can hear an axe ring a mile off when the wind's right. All he had to do was follow the sound in."

I stood there thinking about the whole thing. Why couldn't anybody leave me alone? That was the whole point of coming up into the mountains—to get away from everybody. Just didn't want nobody around. And here come Pa after me, Billings snooping around spying on me. I was getting sore and I slapped myself on the thigh. "Blame it, I wished Pa'd leave me alone."

"I reckon it's what any pa'd do," he said. "Wouldn't leave his son to run wild in the woods if he could help it. Although like I say, I ain't got a lot of experience with Pa's."

"I never saw where he gave a damn for me before," I spit out. "Why's he so fired up to have me back now?"

"Well, I can't say I know your pa real well. Go in and out of the store from time to time is all. But he struck me like a fella who wouldn't of let you know he gave a damn for you even if he did." He gave me a look. "Apples don't fall far from the tree, do they?"

"I never had no reason to give a damn for nobody," I said. I was feeling pretty sore by now.

"Maybe your pa didn't have no reason, neither."

I wished the whole thing hadn't of come up. I wished

he never brought Pa up at all. I was getting to the point where I wanted to start throwing things. "I don't want to talk about it," I said.

"I don't have no reason to talk about it."

"Whyn't he leave me alone? Why's he got to come up here after me?"

"I thought we was going to drop it," he said.

"We are," I said. But my fists was balled up and my teeth was clenched, and I spit out, "I wished I kilt him after all."

"No you don't, Jesse," he said, mighty calm. "You don't wish you kilt nobody. Now simmer down. I got some biscuits left from breakfast we can chew on."

I went on standing there with my fists balled up and my teeth clenched. Then I stooped down, snatched a rock off the ground, and flung it as hard as I could out into the trees. I looked around for something else to throw.

"I said to simmer down, Jesse, before I paddle your tail for you."

"You wouldn't dare."

He laughed. "Oh yes I would. I'm about twice your size and been on my own out here since I was fifteen. I kilt a bear with a Bowie knife once. Blame near chewed my arm off before I got him. I can handle a twelve-year-old boy. Now set while I get them biscuits."

I stared at him. "You been out here since you was fifteen?"

"Yep. Couldn't stand being home no more and run off

just like you did, except I had brains enough to wait until I was big enough to manage. Now set."

"You run off when you was a kid, too?"

"Yep."

"What made you do it?"

"Maybe I'll tell you some day. Now set while I get them biscuits." He went into the cabin and I stood there feeling all confused, and couldn't think straight. In a bit he come out of the cabin carrying the skillet with biscuits in it. There was something else in the skillet. He took it out.

"What's that?"

"Honeycomb," he said. "Picked it up when I was in town. I never knew a boy who didn't like honey."

He got it for me. I set down on the chopping block feeling more confused than ever. I was about to cry, but I put my hands over my face like I was wiping the sweat off and held the tears back, so's only one little sob got away from me. Blame it, he wasn't trying to do me no favors. He liked me.

Chapter Six

We set off after the bear at first light the next morning. We picked up the tracks by Larry's trapline. They wasn't easy to follow, for they tracked across pieces of rock ledge and over the thick layer of leaves on the floor of the woods where his paws wouldn't leave no mark. But the ground was still damp from a rain we had, and being as he weighed maybe four, five hundred pounds, he sunk in pretty deep on soft ground. Sometimes he left scuff marks in the leaves, too, and after he crossed a stream his wet paws'd pick up leaves and turn them over. Even so, we kept losing him. Larry showed me what you did when you lost a track: keep spiraling out in wider and wider circles, one of us in each direction; sooner or later you was bound to pick up something, unless he got spooked and run for it. Bears didn't spook easy, Larry said. Just as likely to come for you as run for it.

We tracked him that way all day, stopping at noon to rest a little and eat some cold biscuits and ham Larry'd stuck in his pouch. When it started to get dark, and we couldn't see tracks no more, we quit. I made a fire and we heated up such biscuits and ham as we had. When we was done eating, Larry took a little piece he'd saved off the honeycomb he gave me, jammed a stick into it, and heated the honey over the fire. "Maybe we can bring him in," he said. "He can smell honey a long way off." We waited, but we didn't hear nothing, and after a while we snuggled down into the leaves as best as we could and went to sleep.

I woke up suddenly. A piece of moon was shining down through an open spot in the leaves overhead and I figured that was what woke me up. But then I heard a thump, and a snuffling sound, and a chill run up my spine. He wasn't but fifteen or twenty feet away. I reached over and jiggled Larry. He raised up his head. "He's out there," I whispered.

He didn't say nothing, but reached out easy for his gun. Then we sat staring into the dark, trying to pick out a shape moving in the patches of moonlight, trying to breath quiet and keep still. The thump come again and a snuffle. We looked toward the sound. There was a shape there, low to the ground. Could be a rock, although I didn't remember no rock there before. There come up a grunt, and the shape rose up. Larry brought the gun to his shoulder and let go. The sound of that sudden wham in the night near knocked me over. The bear grunted and roared. I snatched up my gun. Larry grabbed the barrel. "Don't shoot till I get loaded up again," he said fast and low. "I don't aim to fight no more bears with no Bowie knife again."

So I waited while he loaded. The bear roared again. "All right, let him have it, Jesse." The shape was just a blur in the woods. My heart was going like a drum and my arms was trembling. I let go at the blur. He roared again and tore off in the night, crashing and banging in the woods. After a while there was silence.

"He's gone," Larry said. "But we winged him." There wasn't nothing to do but wait for light. I lay down and tried to sleep, but I was roused up too much. I lay there staring at the moon as it slid off to the west. After a while the sky began to lighten a little. We ate most of the rest of the biscuits and ham and sat there waiting for more light. When the sun began poking splotches of yellow through the trees to the east, we got up and took a look at where the bear'd been. The ground was all tore up, some branches busted, some spots of blood on the leaves covering the ground.

"He'll bleed to death pretty soon, won't he, Larry?" I was mighty hopeful he would.

Larry shook his head. "Maybe not. I seen bears that had four, five old bullets in 'em. Just healed over with the bullet inside 'em."

Truth was, he wasn't bleeding that much. But he was bleeding enough to leave spots on the ground here and there, so he was a lot easier to track than before. We set off after him a pretty good clip, keeping a good look out so's we wouldn't stumble on him laying behind a rock or in a hole somewhere. He had a couple of hours' start on us, and could move pretty quick through the woods; but Larry figured he'd stop here and there when he come across something worth eating—berries, nest of mice, roots, piece of rotten animal a wolf hadn't finished off.

He was heading up the mountain more or less—zigzagging a good deal, but generally upwards. Larry figured his home territory was over the other side, and he'd got over to our side by mistake. "I don't know as I want to follow him all the way over onto the other slope," Larry said. "I don't know that territory real good. Don't want to get myself lost over there again."

To be honest, I wasn't sure I'd of minded if that bear *did* get away from us. Oh, I wanted to be in on a bear hunt all right—mighty nice thing to boast about afterwards. But we hadn't got to the boasting part yet. We shot him twice and he'd walked uphill for three hours with them bullets in him. What if he turned on us and we both took a shot at him—what was we going to do then, fight him with our knives? The best thing was to hope he'd be half dead when we come across him and wouldn't give us no real trouble.

We went on upwards all morning, and when the sun was overhead we ate what was left of the biscuits and ham—a handful each. That was another thing I begun to see about being a mountain man—you had to get used to going hungry from time to time. No way around it, if you was chasing a bear.

We rested a bit and then set off again, but right away we lost his trail in a stream—couldn't pick up no signs of him on the other side of the stream. Did he take to the stream looking for fish, turtles and such? Which way would he of went? Larry went off upstream and I went downstream looking for signs, and blamed if a hundred feet downstream I found him picking blueberries as calm as you please, not more'n twenty feet away from me through the trees.

He seen me the same time I seen him. He stared for a minute and then he turned to face me on all fours. He growled. "Larry," I shouted. "I got him."

I raised up the gun and sighted at his head—couldn't miss at that distance. But I didn't fire, for I wanted Larry to be there to back me up before I took a shot at him. "Larry," I shouted again. "Come quick." My legs were trembling and my heart thumping to beat anything. The bear raised up a little so's its forepaws were off the ground. He growled again. Behind me I heard snapping and rustling in the underbrush. "Where the hell you at, Jesse?"

"Over here. I think he's going to charge."

The bear was raised up a good bit more. Now I had a clear shot at his heart. I sighted it there. The end of the gun barrel was waving back and forth. I took a couple of deep breaths to calm myself and clenched my muscles to stop that blame muzzle from waving.

Larry come up behind me. I kept my eyes glued on the bear. "Take the first shot, Jesse," he said and at the same minute the bear charged. I let go. The wham echoed in my ears and the bear set down backwards on his tail. I began to load again, my hands trembling so much the powder spilled all over the place. The bear wasn't no more than fifteen feet from us. He roared and rolled forward onto his four feet and started for us again. Larry's gun whammed right behind my ear, making me half deaf. The bear sat back again, shaking its head from side to side. Then he growled again. Larry was down on one knee reloading. I was trying to fumble a ball into the barrel, but my hands was shaking so much I kept dropping it onto the ground. The bear rolled forward onto its feet and charged. I dropped the gun and dove off to one side. He roared as he went by me, heading straight for Larry.

Still on my knees, I swung around to look. Larry was lying on his back, his feet kicking into the bear's face, and struggling to get his knife out of his belt. The bear raised up a paw and took a whack at Larry's feet where they was kicking into his face. He snarled, opening his mouth wide. I never saw such teeth in my life—if he got Larry's foot in them teeth he'd chew it off in a minute.

I never remembered doing it—never knew I did it, but then I was on the bear's back, my face buried down in his fur, dusty, old, gamy smell in my nose, swinging my knife again and again into that tough old pelt. It seemed like I been doing it forever. Then I heard a gun go wham. The bear gave out a big sigh and started to flatten down. I jumped clear. He rolled over on his side and lay there.

I stood there trembling all over, looking at the bear and then at Larry. "How'd you get that shot off?" My voice croaked like a frog.

"You took his mind off me when you jumped him.

Then I seen you was messing up the pelt with your knife and I figured I better shoot him while it was still worth something."

I was too scared to laugh, but I grinned. He come up to me, put his arm around my shoulders, and give me a big hug. I put my arms around him and hugged him back. Blame it, if I didn't want to cry all over again, but I didn't, for I just helped to kill a bear and a bear hunter couldn't be blubbering.

We skinned the bear out—leastwise, Larry did with me helping some. Then Larry cut off as much meat as he figured we could carry along with the pelt. "Half hour after we've gone won't be nothing but the skull left," he said. With his gun butt he knocked out some of the bear's front teeth. "Indians use 'em for necklaces and such. I'll trade 'em for some beaver pelts." He bent down and sliced off one of the bear's paws. "Here," he said. "You kill a bear, you get to wear the paw." I tied it to my belt. I had to figure out how to cure it, but even so I felt mighty proud of myself, for anybody who saw that paw'd know I killed a bear.

We started down the mountain, both loaded up pretty good. That pelt alone weighed near fifty pounds, I reckoned. We had to stop to rest a few times, and by nightfall we was still a long way from home. We made a fire and cooked some of that bear meat on sticks—mighty greasy and good—and then we lay down to sleep. We was up at first light in the morning, but it wasn't until noon that we got back to Larry's cabin. Larry showed me how to salt down the meat in a barrel he had. "Salt meat'll keep for months," he said. "Best to save it for winter when times are hard. I'll keep your share here till you get something to store it in." He tipped his head and gave me a look out of the corner of his eyes. "I figure on curing this here bear skin. I ain't got no doubts you know all about curing skins, otherwise I'd say you might watch to see how I done it."

Well, I still wasn't so blame sure I wanted to take favors from nobody—that wasn't my way. But I was feeling so blame good about everything, what with that bear paw hanging from my belt, and a share of bear meat salted away, I couldn't help myself, and I blurted out, "I reckon it might be interesting to see your particular way of it." So I stayed to watch. He went behind the cabin and come back with a bucket of bark chips that was soaking in water. "These here are oak bark, but you can use hemlock, chestnut chips as well, too." He rubbed the stuff into the skin. "You got to keep her moist with this here stuff. Take maybe a month before she's ready." There was some other tips he gave me, too. I was mighty glad to learn, for now I could start earning some money from pelts myself, instead of having them rot on me and stink up the cabin.

So I started off for home, feeling mighty tired, but about as good as I felt since I come up into the mountains—about as good as I felt since before that morning when Pa told me Ma had run off. I started to sing, "Old Susannah, don't you cry for me." It was blame poor singing, but I didn't care, I felt like singing. So I went along through the woods singing, and then I had a piece of luck, for I got so interested in "Old Susannah" I tripped on a root and fell. That shut me up for a minute. And I was lying there on the ground when I heard a voice not fifty feet from me. "That's Jesse singing, I'd recognize him anywhere. He always sung like an owl." It was Pa.

Chapter Seven

I lay low to the ground. How'd Pa know where I was? How'd he figure that out? Knew that Larry seen me from time to time and figured I had to be up somewhere near to where Larry's cabin was. Larry never made no secret about his cabin. I reckoned a lot of fellas knew where it was. Pa could of found out easy enough. Maybe the fella Pa was with knew.

Since I quit singing they dropped their voices down a notch. I couldn't make out what they was saying, but I could hear their voices. Blame it, why'd I have to start singing like that? Didn't I have no sense at all? What kind of a blame fool was I to go through the woods singing "Old Susannah" at the top of my lungs?

I raised my head up a little and looked around. They was down the slope from me, hid in the trees. They knew where I was more or less. They wouldn't come charging up from me—try to slip up on me. I took a look around the woods, studying it as best as I could without raising up my head too high. Off to the left of me a couple hundred feet was a patch of blow-down, big tree trunks laying atop of one another every which way. Couldn't see it, but I knew it was there. Once I got in there amongst that blow-down they wouldn't spot me from five feet away.

But I'd best throw them off first, I figured. So I started sliding forward on my belly, scuffling up the leaves pretty good, and when I figured I'd got far enough away from them so they couldn't see me through the trees I raised up into a crouch and slipped off to the left through the woods until I got to the blow-down. I clambered in there, crawling under tree trunks, climbing over them, until I was in the middle of it. I lay flat behind a big old rotten tree trunk two foot across. They'd never find me in there unless they was standing on top of me. I waited, keeping my breath quiet. I could only pray that they wouldn't go on up the mountain another quarter mile to where my cabin was.

By and by I heard their voices again. "Look here," the fella with Pa said. "He quit crawling and stood up. He must of figured he was out of earshot of us and's making a run for it up the mountain."

"I don't trust it," Pa said. "Jesse's ornery enough, but he's right smart."

That took me by surprise. I always reckoned I was kind of dumb. Didn't have no particular reason to believe that, but I did. Why'd I come to think I was dumb? I didn't know. I was always smarter than Charlie Williams, I reckoned. Still, I always though I was dumb. And here was Pa saying I was right smart.

I lay there, feeling surprised and kind of pleased with myself. Come to think of it, why shouldn't I be smart? What was wrong with it? I had as much right to be smart as anyone else, didn't I?

"I don't know as I'd call it right smart to run off into the mountains, and feed on lizards and snakes when he could be enjoying eggs and bacon back home," the other fella said.

"Oh, he's smart, all right. Couldn't fool him much even when he was a little kid. You couldn't trick him into nothing. Tell him if he didn't eat his cauliflower he'd grow warts on his nose or some such. He'd just say he'd take a chance on it, and if he started to grow warts he'd think about it again. He was smart enough. He laid that there trail on purpose, and went off somewheres else. I'd bet on it."

Why didn't Pa ever say nothing like that before? Whyn't he tell me I was right smart? Didn't I have a right to know? I wished he'd done it.

"Well, you know your boy, I reckon," the fella said. "I still don't see nothing smart about running off into the mountains when he could have been sleeping in a nice warm bed at night."

"That's Jesse. Being ornery gets in your way sometimes. It ain't that he's not smart. Gets that from his ma, I reckon."

That was another one that took me by surprise. I wouldn't of said that Ma was any smarter than Pa was. A whole lot nicer. But I wouldn't of said a whole lot smarter. Pa, he was smart enough. That wasn't the trouble with him.

But if I was like Ma, how come she went off the way she did? I didn't like thinking about that so I closed my eyes and squeezed them shut.

Now the fella with Pa said, "Where'd you think he went to, then?"

"Your guess is as good as mine. He's probably given us the slip. I reckon we best go find this here Larry's cabin. Maybe he's got a line on where Jesse's at. Maybe Jesse's living there. You know where Larry's cabin is?"

"I told you, I been there once, hunting. Got caught in a rainstorm and holed up there for a couple of hours."

"All right, let's go," Pa said.

"What're you going to do with him if you find him? Rope and tie him?"

"See if I can talk some sense into him. I reckon he's getting tired of living rough. I doubt he's had a square meal for a month. Might be he's ready to come back if he got a little encouragement." They didn't say nothing for a minute. Then Pa said, "Well, let's go find this here mountain man."

I wanted to stand up and tell Pa he was wrong. I wasn't tired of living rough at all. I wanted to tell him I took on a bear with a knife and got the paw in my belt to show for it. I wanted to tell them I had a pile of bear meat salted down in a barrel and a share in a bearskin with only four-five knife holes in it. I wanted to tell him I got myself a cabin near built except for the chimney and bark for the roof. I wanted to tell him I could get on mighty well without him, and he ought to be proud of me, instead of thinking I couldn't take it up here in the mountains and was ready to come home. "You ought to be proud of me, Pa," I whispered. "I wished you was."

But I didn't say none of it, just went on laying there in the blow-down, waiting.

I give them a good half hour to get out of range of me. Finally I didn't hear nothing and decided I was clear. I figured I'd best circle back up to my cabin around to the south and come up on it from the back, the uphill side, just in case they stumbled on it somehow. So I clambered to the blow-down opposite from the way I came in.

I been up through this area a couple of times, but I didn't know it real well—had most concentrated on the territory off to the north, towards Larry's cabin. I took my time about getting back. Didn't want to make no more noise than necessary, and wanted to be sure where I was so's I wouldn't get turned around. I came on through the woods a way, heading southwest, and then I turned to go due west up the mountain, so as to climb up higher than my cabin and circle back to it. And I was going along this way when I saw ahead of me one of them clearings you come onto in the woods, nice patch of grass with the sun shining onto it and a little breeze stirring the grass. When I come to the edge of it I crouched down, making sure there wasn't nobody in sight before I crossed it. For a minute I crouched there. Then the breeze ran across the grass, bending it over like a hand brushing through a cat's fur, and swept across the clearing to the woods on the other side. I knew the bad feeling was coming. The knots came into my stomach, my muscles clenched up, the skin across the top of my head grew tight. I was back in that place—barn, shed, whatever it was—all by myself, staring out across the field to the woods below where something bad was happening. I raised my arm up, sighted down it at the woods across. "Bang," I whispered. The noise shook me out of myself. I took a deep breath and jumped up, shaking my arms and legs so's to get the picture out of my head. Then I set off for home, skirting around that clearing of grass like it was full of snakes. After that I circled around behind my cabin and sat up there in the woods for a while, watching. But nobody was there, and I went on down. I was mighty tired all right. I ate some cold biscuits and honey and went to sleep. I was ready for it.

It worried me some the next morning that Pa might still be up in the mountains, and might track me down. But nobody come around, and finally I figured that Pa must of gone home yesterday before darkness come on. So I went to work carrying big sheets of loose bark from the blow-down, laying them up on my roof poles and weighing them down with rocks. It was the kind of job that didn't take much thought and left me room to think about myself. Did Pa and that fella catch up to Larry? Found his cabin, I reckoned, but maybe Larry wasn't there. Maybe they waltzed around for a while and then went back down the mountain. Maybe that was all there was to it.

But suppose they did? What was they saying about me? Finally I couldn't stand it no more. I washed up a little in the brook, picked up my gun, and went off around the mountain to Larry's place.

Larry was in front of the cabin, sawing up the firewood. He stopped sawing, and let the blade rest in the saw cut. "I figured you'd show up soon enough. I knew you wouldn't be able to sit still until you satisfied your curiosity."

"I got a right to be curious, he's my own pa."

"I didn't say you didn't have a right. I just said you was curious."

I was trying to keep myself from getting sore, especially with Larry. "Well, I was," I said. "What'd Pa want?"

"You ought to be able to figure that out for yourself. He wanted to know where you was."

"You didn't tell him."

He gave me a look. "You think I would of?"

I blushed for I shouldn't of doubted him. "No, I trusted that you wouldn't."

"Told him I seen you around from time to time. Said you was living in a lean-to for a while, but you moved further off and wasn't in no hurry to let people know where you was living. I figured that was all true enough. I don't like lying to nobody."

"That's all you talked about?" The funny thing was, I was disappointed. Here I was fuming and fretting over them talking about me, and then when I find out maybe they wasn't talking about me after all, I got disappointed. That didn't make no sense.

Larry took the saw out of the saw cut and laid it careful against a log so as not to spoil the edge. Then he sat down on the chopping block and looked at me. "He wants you to come home real bad, Jesse. He said you wasn't big enough to take care of yourself in the woods, yet."

"I did pretty good so far," I said.

"He said he was worried what you'll do this winter. Get caught in deep snow and get chewed up by a hungry mountain jack." He looked at the ground. "That's what he says, anyway. I reckon there's more to it than that."

"Like what?"

He looked at me. "I reckon you can figure that out for yourself."

I didn't say anything for a minute. I was beginning to lose a hold of myself and I knew I shouldn't do that to Larry. "If he wants me back so bad, why didn't he do nothing to keep me there?"

"It ain't his style. He ain't one for handing out the compliments. I reckon now he wishes he had."

The itchy, scratchy feeling was growing in me. I took a deep breath to run some air over it. "I'm his son. He might of taken that into account." I looked away. "Was his son, anyway."

"Jesse, you got to keep it in mind, the whole fault don't lie with him. You can be might ornery when you put your mind to it."

The hot scratchy feeling was growing and I knew I was about to start throwing stuff. "I reckoned you'd be on my side," I said.

He looked at me for a while. Then he said, "Now, Jesse, you just calm yourself down before you do something you're sorry for."

"I am calm," I said. "I ain't riled up." I looked around for something to throw.

"Your fist is balled up and you got a face on you like that bear when he come after us."

I raised up my hands and looked at them. They was clenched so tight my fingernails was digging into my skin. I took a deep breath and unclenched. "I'm calmed down now," I said. I took another deep breath.

He didn't say nothing, but stood up. "I got to get a drink of water," he said.

But that wasn't it. He was giving me time to get a hold of myself. He picked up his tin cup that was lying on the block the turtle shell sat on, and scooped some water out of the shell. He took a drink. He filled the tin cup again and held it out to me. "Want some?"

"No."

He went on holding the cup out. I took the cup and gulped down some water. "I'm calmed down now," I said. "I won't throw nothing."

Larry sat down on the chopping block again. "See, here's the way I look at it, Jesse. Most usually I try to stay out of other people's way. Don't like taking sides. It never does nobody no good, not them, not you. I can see your side of it, Jesse, but I reckon your pa's got a side of it, too. Right now you ain't gonna listen to his side, and wouldn't hear it if you did listen. But maybe someday you will. If you want my opinion, which you probably don't, maybe you ought to go down there and talk to him. It won't do you no harm. He can't keep you down there less'n he ropes and ties you, and he ain't gonna do that." He held up one finger. "Now, I ain't *recommending* you should do it. I'm just saying maybe you ought to give it some thought."

"No," I said, shaking my head. "Never. For certain. I don't care what his blame side is to it. He can go his way and I'm going to go mine."

Larry shrugged. "It ain't no skin off my nose. Don't mind saying I like having a little company dropping by the cabin from time to time. Takes off the loneliness." He stood up and dusted the subject off his hands. "Now I got to take a look at my trapline. Don't want to leave some animal suffering no more than I have to. You want to come along, or you feeling too ornery?"

I was feeling ornery all right and not much like smiling, but I managed to pull my lips back a little. "I'll come along," I said.

Chapter Eight

I was tired of everybody saying I was ornery. I didn't think I was ornery as they said. Some ornery, maybe, I had to give them that, for there was them times when I lost hold of myself. But I was only ornery sometimes.

So what if I was ornery, anyway? What business was it of theirs? Look at Pa, he could be blame ornery hisself. He didn't have no right telling anybody else they was ornery. Did I get it from him? I hoped not. I didn't want to get anything from Pa. Rather take after Ma. Pa said I got smart from Ma, if I was smart, which a lot of times I wasn't so sure about. I didn't mind taking after Ma. She wasn't ornery. Not as I remembered her anyway. Five years since she left. I was only seven and most likely didn't know the truth of her anyway. But she wasn't ornery, I was sure of that. Used to say poems to me when she put me to bed. She knew a slew of poems. One about "The Boy Stood on the Burning Deck." "Paul Revere's Ride" of course. She could say the whole thing right through, although I couldn't be sure of that, because I usually fell asleep halfway through.

Ma was always on me about speaking right—didn't let me say "ain't" and such. She said her and Pa didn't have much education and she wanted me to have some. Pa said my speech got a whole lot worse since she left. Wouldn't doubt it neither: Pa didn't stay on me about it the way she done. Pa said it come from hanging around with Charlie Williams, but I never saw where his speech was a lot worse than mine was. We was like peas in a pod, Charlie's ma always said.

Ma liked having me help in the kitchen. Stir the cake dough in her big yellow bowl, wash up the pots and pans, mash the spuds with her big wooden masher. She always said I was a big help to her. Don't reckon I was, how much use can a four-five-six-year-old kid be? But I believed it then. She said she liked having me around. Gave her someone to chitchat with. I guess Pa wasn't much of a one for chitchat. Come to think of it, I guess Ma must have been lonely for company a lot of the time. Oh, she had her friends, I reckon. Used to go over and sit with Widow Wadman sometimes. Sit in the shade of Widow Wadman's porch doing her sewing, the two of them side by side on a bench. Sometimes I'd play out in the yard while they talked, scratching designs in the dirt with a stick, or pretending I was a hunter on a horse chasing buffalo. Widow Wadman done most of the talking. Ma, she wasn't much of a talker, I guess. Come to think of it, probably she was a little bit shy. Except with me. She liked for me to come into the kitchen and sit on her high stool and chitchat. She used to tell me all kinds of stories about what it was like when she was a kid back there in Pennsylvania. They had a little old farm up towards Lake Erie somewheres. Six kids in the family, all close in age. Three boys and three girls. Ma was in the middle, a girl and two boys ahead of her. Didn't have much money, Ma said, but they had lots of fun, a whole bunch of brothers and sisters running around together, swimming in the creeks in summer, sliding down hills in winter, roasting apples in the fireplace on cold October nights when the apples was ripe, laughing and shouting. Plenty of work, too, Ma said, to feed all them children, but you was always working with some of the others and could sing together, tell stories, or josh each other back and forth to make the time go by. That was why she didn't get much schooling—too much work around the farm. Her own ma, my grandma what was, tried her best to teach them writing and ciphering and such, but it only went so far. That was where Ma learned all of them poems—Grandma made all the kids learn a new poem from time to time. I forgot what the reason for it was, but the one who learned their poem best got a prize—pretty handkerchief, ribbons for a bonnet if it was a girl, Barlow knife or some such if it were a boy. Ma said she was good at memorizing poems and got a lot of handkerchiefs. Lost 'em along the way somehow. Wished she had been more careful. Even when I was a little kid I could tell she missed those old times. The family was all broke up and scattered now. She didn't even know where some of them was, but she wrote back and forth a little to one of her sisters she was closest in age to, and managed to keep up with the family some. I always wanted to meet them. It seemed like they must be a nice bunch to be around. I wished I had a lot of brothers and sisters. Sometimes I used to dream about me and Ma going back to Pennsylvania to meet them. Of course I had to stop that kind of dreaming when Ma ran off from us.

Well, anyways, I couldn't of got ornery from Ma. Maybe I was just ornery from nature. Just born that way, and couldn't help myself. So what if I was ornery? That was my business, wasn't it? Why shouldn't I be ornery if I wanted to? That was me. That was who I was in a nutshell.

Finally I got tired of mooning over myself and quit it. I been keeping an eye on some blueberry bushes that was getting ripe, so as to get there before the birds did. I decided to go have a look at them to take my mind off myself. So I went along the side of the mountain to where they was growing, four high-bush blueberries about six feet tall. The berries was getting ripe, some still green, but a good many of them fat and juicy. I took off my shirt, tied up the sleeves to make bags out of them, and set to work. I picked away, feeling the sun hot on my bare back and for once not thinking of anything but what a pretty day it was—dragonflies humming by, orange butterfly here and there, birds atwittering around me, sore that I was getting the blueberries ahead of them. Then I began to get the feeling that something was watching me.

I didn't know where that feeling come from. Maybe I

seen something flash out of the corner of my eye—
branch moving when there wasn't no breeze or something. Maybe I heard a little noise, a click, like a stone got
kicked. Didn't know what it was, but I had that feeling
and a shiver went up my back. The prettiness went out of
the day, like a cloud coming over the sun.

I stretched my arms out like I was yawning and turned
slowly around, like I didn't have anything particular on
my mind but easing my back. I gave the woods a quick
sweep with my eyes. Nothing. Not a blame thing. If it of
been a bear I'd of seen it. Brown fur blends in with the
trees pretty good, but on a sunny day I'd of seen it anyway. Mountain jack was another question. Seen one in
the distance a couple of times, but if it was up a tree, or
flattened out in the grass, you might miss it.

I gave my eyes another swing across the woods, and
then I turned back to the blueberry bush. I put my
hands inside the bush like I was picking, and stood dead
still, listening. And in half a minute I heard a soft little
thump, and I knew it wasn't no animal out there, it was
a human being. My skin crawled worse than ever.

But I kept a hold of myself and started picking berries
again, for so long as I didn't give no sign I knew he was
there he wasn't likely to jump me. Or run, whichever he
had in mind. I picked my way slowly around the berry
bush like I didn't have nothing in mind but picking it
clean. As I went around I kept looking through the bush
into the woods beyond. I couldn't see much through
the bush's leaves. So when I was half around I stopped

picking, turned around, so as to scratch my back on the blueberry bush, and studied the woods in front of me. Nothing. Nobody. I could see a good fifty feet into the woods. If anyone'd been there, he wasn't there no more.

Still, I didn't trust it. I yawned again, picked up my gun where I'd left it leaning into the berry bush, and lay down in the shade at the edge of the woods. I took out my handkerchief and stretched it across my eyes, like I was keeping the sun out. But I kept my eyes open, for you can see through a handkerchief, especially an old wore out one like mine, when it's close to your eyes. I lay there, all nerved up, listening for sounds of him creeping in on me. I was having the hardest time keeping my arms and legs from twitching. Finally I couldn't stand it no longer. I got up, tucked the handkerchief in my pocket, and went off real careful into the woods where I figured that sound come from, studying the ground. In about a minute I saw a long scuff mark in the leaves and at the end of the scuff mark a heel print. It wasn't hard to figure: he'd skidded on the leaves until his foot hit the dirt and sunk in. When he skidded, either he thumped his gun butt on the ground, thumped his hand against a tree to steady himself, thumped something. It was clear as day what happened. Probably he slipped hisself back into the woods right afterwards, like as not cussing hisself out for being clumsy.

Who was it? Not Pa. He'd have walked right up and tried to talk some sense into me. Couldn't be Larry. He didn't have no reason to spy on me, for he could ask me anything he wanted and I'd of told him. Would of told him where my cabin was if he asked, although he wasn't likely to.

Who then? Somebody Pa sent up who knew the mountains better than he did? Somebody to follow me back to my cabin, and then go on down and tell Pa about it? That seemed more likely.

Whoever it was, somebody was spying on me. It made me feel mighty uneasy. There was a dangerous feeling to it, for I didn't know what they was planning on doing to me. Just something dangerous out there and nothing I could do about it.

I wasn't going to lead him back to my cabin, for certain, so I headed over to Larry's cabin. Even as I was coming up I heard Larry's saw going *whirr, whirr* in the wood. When I come into the clearing he stopped sawing and stood with the blade in the cut and his hand resting on the handle. "Hello, Jesse," he said. He took out his handkerchief with his left hand and swabbed off his face.

"Somebody's up here spying on me," I said.

He looked at me. "You sure? You got a pretty good imagination for such things, Jesse."

"It wasn't no imagination. I seen a footprint. Heel print. I was picking blueberries up behind the gorge and I heard something. When I went to look I seen the heel print." I was embarrassed to tell him about laying there with the handkerchief over my eyes. Now that I was talking to him I seen right away that he'd think it was a mighty dumb thing to do.

"Could have been your own heel. Made it when you went in there."

"Too big."

He pulled the saw out of the log and slanted it against another log so the teeth was off the ground. "Who do you reckon it was?"

"Somebody Pa sent. Planned to track me to my cabin so's Pa could find me."

"How you reckon whoever it was found you up there in that blueberry patch? One boy in ten square miles of mountain? It'd be like finding a nickel at the bottom of a lake."

"I don't know. Maybe he was up here hunting a lot, and knows where things are."

"Ain't blame likely even so. If I was to go looking for you I'd have a hard time of it, and I know this here territory like the back of my hand. Nobody from town'd find you in a month of Sundays, less'n you was wandering around singing."

"I learned my lesson about 'Old Susannah,'" I said. "Well, Larry, what do you make of it then?"

"Nothing, maybe," he said. "All it come down to was you heard a noise and seen a heelprint. There's all kind of things can make a noise in the woods—tree squeaking in the wind, dead branch falling, little animal scuttling along. All kind of things."

"What about the heel print?"

"Fella could of went in there last week for all you know. If it *was* a footprint. Could have been a place where an animal kicked up a stone. Deer'd do that with them hooves."

"There was a skid mark on the leaves coming up to it."

"Still could have been a deer." He squinted a little. "That's one thing I learned, Jesse, don't jump to conclusions too quick. Now, I ain't saying you're wrong. Maybe it was some fella spying on you. Could have been, knowing how bad your Pa wants you back. But I tell you, Jesse, people can get theirselves to believe most anything if they want to bad enough. That's another thing I learned. I swear, people can get themselves to believe the blamedest things. Believe they're gonna be rich as soon as their luck changes, even though they ain't had nothing but bad luck for fifty years. Believe their children is saints when the little girl don't like nothing better than setting fire to cats and the boy gets his liquor money breaking open church boxes. Human bein's can believe anything they set their mind to."

"Why would I want to believe Pa sent somebody up here after me?"

Larry squinted at me again. "That's a interesting question, ain't it?"

"Well, it don't fit my case. I don't want Pa up here talking sense into me."

"We haven't decided he comes into it at all."

He was forcing me to think about it. What if he was right? I wasn't going on very much, just a thump that I might of misheard and a heel print. Still, I was certain of it. I remembered how I felt out there, with my back all shivery. How could a feeling like that be wrong? Still, maybe it was. "I don't want to take a chance on it," I said.

He nodded. "Well, I can see that. But I'm telling you, it wasn't nobody from town. Couldn't of found you in a month of Sundays."

"Who, then?"

"Well, if it was a human being, which I ain't convinced of yet, it had to be somebody who knows his way around the mountains. Had to be somebody who knows the territory."

"Billings."

"The thought crossed my mind."

That worried me. "Do you think he found my cabin?"

"If it was him, no. He wouldn't of been spying on you if he already knew where your cabin was. He could find you up there most nights if he wanted to. But there's other fellas in the mountains it might have been, too. You got to remember, a lot of these fellas don't care to see no more folks up here than necessary. For one thing, they don't see no reason for sharing the pelts with nobody. For another, they wouldn't of come up here in the first place if they liked having a lot of folks around."

"Is that why Billings is so all-fired against me? He just don't like having people around? Whyn't he just stay away from me, then?"

"*If* it was him out there. Maybe he don't like kids in particular. I met people like that." He paused for a minute and looked off into the woods, like he was seeing something out there. "Don't like their own kids, some 'em. Blame hard on a kid growing up that way."

That idea gave me a kind of funny, itchy feeling. Was that why Ma run off from us? She didn't like me? I didn't see how that could be true, not all them times she let me lick the cake spoon and told me poems to put me to sleep. "Maybe that's what's wrong with Pa. He don't like kids."

"No, I wouldn't say that, Jesse. He wouldn't be going to all this trouble to get you back if he didn't like kids. Leave you up here to get et by a mountain jack instead."

"Even so, maybe he don't like kids."

"I'd of took your pa over some I knew, Jesse." He scratched his chin. "Now here's another question. Suppose your pa put Billings on you?"

The idea took me by surprise. "You think Pa would of done that?"

"Well, he knows Billings. Don't know as they been great pals, but I seen Billings down there in the store from time to time chewing the fat with your pa like they was friendly. If it was me, I'd of asked Billings what it'd be worth to see if he could find your cabin, and take me up there. Give Billings a nice saw, flitch of ham, a little credit at the store in exchange."

We didn't neither of us say anything for a minute.

Then I said, "What do you think I ought to do, Larry?"

"I already told you what I reckoned you ought to consider."

I thought for a minute. "You mean go down and talk to Pa."

"I ain't giving you no advice, mind, Jesse. I never seen where it done any good to give people advice. If they was likely to take it." He thought for a minute. "I just want to remind you, this Billings ain't no pussycat setting by the fire meowing for his dish of milk."

Chapter Nine

I wasn't in no rush to leave Larry, but I didn't want to admit I was scared, neither, and finally I said good-bye and left. In case he was out there following me, I didn't head for the cabin, but set off on a course that cut along the mountain below where the cabin was. I was mighty nervous and tensed up, and stopped dead about every two minutes to listen for a branch whipping or a thump of some kind. Finally I realized I couldn't go wandering around in the woods all night. Most likely I was imagining things and there was nobody out there. So I went on home to the cabin.

But I didn't sleep too good that night. Woke up every little while, my heart ripping along, thinking somebody was creeping around the cabin. Sometimes it was a field mouse or a squirrel scratching at the walls, or an owl hooting. Sometimes it wasn't nothing at all. I'd go back to sleep, and wake up again an hour later, my heart beating like a drum, my ears perked up for some sound that didn't come.

I felt better in the morning when the daylight brought some common sense into things. I had plenty to do to keep my mind off my worries—snares to check, water to bring up to the cabin, deer trails to look over for fresh prints. Still, I couldn't get it out of my mind that somebody was out there in the woods, laying behind a tree or a rock, watching me. Finally I got to where I couldn't stand it anymore: I just had to find out.

So I picked up my gun and headed down the mountainside for the blueberry bushes where he was spying on me before. I picked it pretty clean the day before, but that time of the year there was always new berries coming along; and besides, he wouldn't rightly know whether there was ripe berries on the bushes or not.

I leaned my gun into the bushes where I could grab it real quick, and then I started to sing "Old Susannah," as loud as I could without using up my voice right away. I sang the whole thing through as best as I could remember it—got some of the words tangled up here and there, but I reckoned that wouldn't matter to whoever was out there. When I got through the whole thing I quit for a while and listened, picking my way around the bush so's I could take a look into the woods in all directions. Didn't hear nothing, didn't see nothing. So I went back to singing until my voice tired out, and listened some more. Still nothing.

Maybe Larry was right. Maybe there was nobody out there after all. Maybe a deer made that scuff mark on the leaves the way Larry said. Thinking that relieved me a good deal, and I sort of relaxed a little. But blame me if I wasn't a touch disappointed, too. Why on earth would I feel disappointed that nobody was coming after me?

It didn't make no sense at all. Still, it was a relief. Just to make sure I decided to give it one more chance. So I busted into singing "Old Susannah" again. I went on for a while until I started to get hoarse. I figured that ought to do it. I'd been out there at that blueberry bush for a good three-quarters of an hour. Anybody within earshot who wanted to find me would have got there by now.

So I started to pick at what berries there was left and I hadn't hardly been at it for a minute when I heard behind me a kind of rustling sound. My back went cold and I froze dead still. Half of me wanted to snatch up my gun and run out of there as fast as I could move. But I kept control of myself, and made my hands move around in the bush like I was picking. I give that a minute. Then I yawned, stretched, picked up my gun, and sauntered easy halfway around the berry bush until I was looking through the bush into the woods where the rustling sound come from. Hanging onto the gun with one hand I pushed some of the blueberry branches aside to clear out my view a little. Straight ahead through the bush, not fifty feet into the woods, there was a flat lump on the ground, like a log. But there wasn't no log there when I come in. I began to sing, "Oh don't you cry for me," and as soon as I started the bump moved and just for a couple of seconds I seen a face.

My hands was trembling, my guts was cold, and my legs was weak, for I was about to stand up to a grown man. I wished I was anyplace but there—wished Larry would come whistling along, wished a bear come lumbering out of the woods, wished anything. But I didn't have no choice. I slid the gun up and slipped it through the blueberry bush. Then I said good and loud, trying to keep my voice from trembling, "I got you in my sights." I took a deep breath so as to calm down a little. "Stand up out of there real slow."

He didn't move, didn't make a sound, but went on laying there. Was it all my imagination again? Was it just a log laying there after all? "Don't give me that. I see you plain as a day."

Still nothing. The seconds ticked by. Blame it, it couldn't be a log, I seen that face. I took another deep breath. Then I jerked the gun out of the blueberry bush and jumped out into the clear. The second I done it he was up on his knees fumbling in the leaves behind him. I dropped to one knee and sighted down the barrel, aiming for his chest.

He flung his hands up. "Hang on," he shouted. "Don't shoot."

I went on kneeling with the gun still aimed at his chest. "Come on out of there on your knees real slow. If you try to stand I'm going to shoot you."

"Hold your fire, Jesse. I ain't gonna do nothing." He come forward on his knees until he was out of the woods and into the little clearing around the blueberry bushes, where I could see him good. He was a lanky fella, tall, as much as I could tell with him still on his knees. He had a red beard, wearing a pair of Indian moccasins, deerskin shirt. Thirty-five, forty years old. Been in the mountains a long time, I reckoned.

I stood up, still holding the gun on him, and looked him over some more. He had a good-sized knife in his belt, but no pistol I could see. Slowly I circled around him, all the while keeping the gun sighted on his chest. When I got into the woods where he'd been laying I fumbled around in the leaves with my feet until I hit something solid. Quickly I bent and snatched up the gun from the ground. Now I had two shots at him and he knew it.

I leaned his gun against my side and lowered mine, but held it across in front of me. I had him now, but what was I going to do with him? I wished I'd of thought that through beforehand. "You this here Billings?" I said.

"That's what they call me."

"What've you been spying on me for?"

He didn't say nothing.

"Did my pa send you after me?"

"What do you think?" he said.

He didn't say nothing for a little bit. Then he said, "It's for your own good, Jesse. You ain't big enough yet. You're bound to freeze to death when winter comes, go out floundering in the snow and get chewed up by a bobcat that can't find nothing better to eat. Go on home to your pa until you get a little more heft on you. It's for your own good. You ain't big enough yet."

He was treating me like he was the grown-up and I was just a kid who didn't know nothing about anything.

It was making me sore—I had the gun on him, didn't I? I was supposed to be the boss here. "I done pretty good so far, Billings."

"Sure, but you ain't seen winter up here yet. You got no idea what it's like. A lot of fellas clear out in the winter." He stopped for a minute. Then he said, "Tell you what, Jesse, you go on home like I said and I'll keep an eye on your cabin for you. Keep it safe. When you get a little bigger it'll be waiting for you."

He better stop treating me like a little kid. "These ain't your damn mountains. I got a right to be here."

"It ain't safe for you, Jesse." He shifted his legs around. "Mind if I stand up, Jesse. My legs is getting a little cramped."

He was beginning to rile me up. "No. You just stay right where you are."

Suddenly he stared into my face. "Hey, go easy, Jesse. Don't get all riled up about it."

"I ain't getting riled up," I said. But I was—was getting into the mood where I wanted to throw something, except that I was holding a gun.

"Just be calm," he said. "Nothing to get riled up about."

I didn't like him telling me to stay calm neither. "I'll get riled up if I want."

"Sure," he said. "I ain't telling you what to do. You got the drop on me. Nothing I can do about it."

"Did Pa tell you not to rile me up? What'd he say to

you about it?" There they were talking about me again.

"Jesse, he didn't say nothing at all to me about it."

"You're lying, Billings." I was feeling mighty scratchy. I wished I had something to throw but I had the gun in my hands. "You was talking to him about me."

He was sweating now and he raised his sleeve to wipe off his forehead. "Jesse, nobody had to tell me nothing. Everybody in town knew what you done to him when you was riled up."

"That ain't none of your business. That's between me and Pa."

He took a deep breath. "Now look, Jesse, your poor pa wants you to come home something fierce. I wouldn't have tracked after you if he hadn't of asked."

"You wasn't tracking after me. You was spying. You wanted to find out where my cabin was." My hands was clenched tight around the gun stock and I felt scratchy all over.

"Jesse, your pa just wanted to know if you was all right. Wanted me to keep an eye on you. That's the truth, Jesse. I swear it."

"I don't believe it. You was trying to find my cabin."

He took another deep breath. "Now look, Jesse, just be calm. Your poor pa loves you. He's mighty worried about you and—"

I swung my gun up to my shoulder and without even bothering to sight I pulled the trigger. There was the most awful wham, but even as the gun was going off I knew I'd jerked the barrel just a little off to one side, and Billings was running through the woods as fast as I ever seen anyone move through trees. I stood there holding the gun, shaking and trembling, all the fight gone out of me. All I could think was, thank God I pulled the muzzle of the gun aside, or that fella'd be lying dead in front of me, and I'd of been feeling just awful and wishing I was dead myself. I don't know why I did it. Couldn't remember what was going through my mind, couldn't really remember doing it until there come that terrible wham. Oh, thank God I pulled that muzzle aside. And I knew one thing: I had to quit letting things rile me up so, for one day I was going to kill someone, certain.

Chapter Ten

I had to talk to Larry about it. Wanted to tell him in the worst way. I went over to his cabin as quick as I could. He wasn't there. I sat down on his chopping block to wait for him. Then it came to me I made a pretty good target sitting there, so I went into the cabin and sat on Larry's bed with the two guns across my lap, feeling rotten, and mighty sick of myself. I sat there like that the whole afternoon. There was some biscuits on a pan on the table. I broke off a piece of biscuit, and chewed on it, but I couldn't swallow it down. Finally I went into the yard and spit it out.

Larry showed up just after dark. When I heard him come out of the woods I went to the cabin door. When he seen me he stopped. "You look like you lost your best friend."

I wished my feelings didn't show so clear on my face. "I come near to killing that fella Billings," I said.

He gave me a look. "Did you? How'd that come about?"

"I told you somebody was tracking me. It was him."

"Well now," he said. We went into the cabin and sat, me on his bed, him on his bench, and I told him the whole thing—how I'd lured Billings into the blueberry bushes by singing, how I'd got the drop on him, how he'd riled me up by treating me like a kid, talking about Pa wanting me back and such, until I couldn't hang onto myself no more and took a shot at him. "I couldn't of missed, not from that distance, but I did. Pulled the muzzle aside when I pulled the trigger."

He looked at me for a bit and I looked down at my shoes. "What made you pull the muzzle aside?"

I wanted to say I never had no idea of shooting him in the first place, I was just trying to throw a scare into him. But I couldn't say it—couldn't lie to Larry somehow. Wouldn't have sounded right in my ears. "Blamed if I know," I said. "Maybe I got some sense at the last minute."

He shook his head. "You was mighty lucky you didn't shoot him, Jesse. It would have gone mighty hard with you if you did. Some of these fellas would have thrown you off a cliff and leave the animals to clean you up."

I swallowed. "They would of?"

"Likely to unless you had a blame good excuse."

"He was spying on me. I know I shouldn't of took a shot at him, but he was spying on me. He shouldn't of done that neither. It riled me up."

"No, he shouldn't of. He didn't have no business spying on you. You got a right to be riled up at him. But taking a shot at him was foolishness. Billings, he's gonna tell everybody up here you're dangerous—a wild animal who ain't got any control over yourself. After that anyone wants to take a shot a you, all they got to do is say you got out of control and they had to shoot you in self-defense. They all know what happened with your pa. And now this. You wouldn't have a leg to stand on."

That was mighty scary. "You think he'll come after me—likely shoot me?"

"If he got any sense, no. But he might. Maybe he figures he's got to kill you before you kill him. He killed a man out there in California. Or so they say."

"But I didn't shoot him. I pulled the muzzle aside." I wished I could remember why I done that. It'd make me feel a whole lot better if I remembered doing it just to throw a scare into Billings. But I couldn't remember.

"Billings ain't likely to believe that. More likely to believe you just plain missed." He looked at me for a minute. "Jesse, you got to stop getting so riled up all the time. It ain't doing you no good. Nor anyone else neither."

I hung my head down and looked at my shoes. "I know, Larry, I'm trying to." But I knew I wasn't.

"Not trying very damn hard so far as I can see."

I kept on looking at my shoes. "I know."

"The least thing Billings'll do is try to run you out of the mountains. Make your life so miserable you'll be glad to get back to town."

I went on looking at my shoes. Finally I didn't want to feel ashamed of myself anymore, so I raised my head up. "I got to talk to him, then. I got to bring him his gun back, anyways."

Larry squinted, the way he done when he wasn't sure

about something. "He's likely to take a shot at you when he sees you coming, Jesse. Maybe I better talk to him."

I wouldn't of liked nothing better. The idea of tracking Billings down and talking to him was real scary. Anything to get out of it. But I couldn't have Larry do it for me. Not and look myself in the eye no more. "I got myself into this mess. I guess I better get myself out of it."

I was kind of hoping he'd say no, he'd do it, but he didn't. "Well, I reckon that's right. Maybe it'll learn you not to get so riled up next time."

"I reckon. I hope so."

"Now Jesse, you be mighty careful of yourself, hear?" Then he told me where Billings had his cabin, somewheres ten miles to the northwest around another corner of the mountain. "Never seen it myself, but some fella I run into once seen it and give me a rough idea of it. You'll see a knob sticking up out of the mountain. It's down under that somewheres. You'll see it once you get up in there. Less'n he sees you first."

I dragged myself off towards my cabin, feeling mighty worried and wondering why I ever wanted to be a mountain man in the first place. It would have been blame easy to pick up my tools, walk down out of the mountains and tell Pa I wanted to come home. Easiest thing in the world to do that. Just walk on out of there and forget about the whole thing. Maybe I wasn't cut out to be a mountain man after all. Maybe I was meant to be a town fella, spend my life keeping Pa's store.

But I knew in my heart I wasn't going to do most of

them things. No matter what, I was going to stay up there in the mountains. Set my heart on it when I was a little kid. Had a start on it now and wasn't going to quit. I had to get myself out of trouble one way or another.

So I walked along, trying to think what I'd say to him when I found him. Tell him I was sorry, was only trying to throw a scare into him and the gun went off by accident? Tell him I wanted to be friends and get along with everybody up there? And I was thinking all of this so hard that I was only twenty feet from the cabin before I saw the deer guts laying in my doorway. Billings found my cabin and left me a calling card. He meant to run me off the mountain. The whole thing was clear as if he writ me a letter. I didn't have no choice no longer. Either I talked to him, or I might as well make up my mind to be a storekeeper for the rest of my life.

I ate some supper and went to sleep, and when I woke up in the morning I was feeling a little braver. Not exactly frolicsome over what lay ahead of me, but game for it. Just bringing his gun back to him was bound to improve his opinion of me. So I ate some breakfast, filled my pouch with some cold biscuits and salt meat, picked up his gun, and set off. I'd of rather taken my gun, too, so as to have a weapon for the trip home, but toting two guns through the woods would have been mighty awkward.

It was going to take me a good long day to get up into Billings' territory, and maybe part of another day by the time I found his cabin. I took my direction from the sun. The first part was territory I knew, and I didn't have no trouble with it, for I knew where to skirt around gorges and cliffs, knew where the streams were shallow and I could ford them easily. Mighty pretty, with red, yellow, blue birds flashing through the trees, patches of blue sky showing through the green leaves, red squirrels going *crek-crek-crek* in the trees—mighty cheerful and pretty if I hadn't of been so worried about what was ahead of me.

After a while I got into strange country where I never been before, and didn't know nothing about. I'd come to a gorge, rocks tumbling down into a stream, and wouldn't know where was the easy way down. Walk along it in one direction hoping to see a deer trail down to the water, and if I didn't come across nothing, clamber down the rocks, hanging onto the gun with one hand and the rocks with the other, praying I wouldn't catch the trigger on a piece of brush and blow my own leg off.

Once down at the bottom I'd have to find a way across the stream rushing along through the boulders, twisting and crashing along, throwing up foamy branches. Worth your life to slip on them wet rocks and fall in—water'd bang you around from rock to rock until you was all broke up or drowned, whichever come first. So I'd walk upstream and downstream looking for a place where the gorge widened out and the water shallowed and slowed down. Sometimes there'd be a tree fell across the stream I could straddle. But sometimes it took a half hour before I found a way across a stream.

Billings, he knew them places already, and could make

good time going in and out of his territory. I didn't, and had to search them out. Between one thing and another, by noon time I knew I wasn't hardly halfway there. Take me the rest of the day to get somewheres near Billings' blame knob, and who knew how long to find his cabin after that. I reckoned I better go easy on food. Didn't want to risk shooting anything, for fear Billings'd hear the shot and come after me. So I et a couple of biscuits and a mouthful of salt meat, rested a while, and set off again, struggling up and down gorges, through briar patches, across streams. I was getting scratched up pretty fair, and had got whipped in the face by branches a half dozen times. The sweat dripped into the scratches, making them sting. My arms and legs was tired. By the time the sun started to go down over the mountain to my left I was blame glad to call it quits for the day. Found a little stream that wasn't moving too fast, stripped down, and plunged in. That water was as cold as ice and stung those scratches like blazes. But it eased the aches in my muscles, and I felt a good deal better when I come out. I lay on the grass by the stream in the last of the sun coming over the mountain until I was warm and dry. Then I got dressed, et all but one of the biscuits, curled up in the grass with my hand on the gun, and went fast asleep. I didn't stir until the sun come shining through the leaves into my face.

I opened my eyes and stared upward. It was going to be a nice day, at least that. I yawned and stretched, wiggling around a little. Then I sat up.

Billings was sitting on a fallen tree about twenty feet away from me, a gun on his knees pointing straight into my face. "Shoe's on the other foot, ain't it, Jesse," he said.

Chapter Eleven

My heart jumped and I sat there staring at him. He's gonna kill me, I thought. He already killed a fella out in California when he caught him alone in the woods, and now he'd caught me alone. I wished I'd never come up into the mountains; I wished I never seen a mountain man. In five minutes I was going to be sprawled out dead. Blame it, I was going to be dead. I could hardly believe it. I felt froze all over. Dying was a big thing. Too important for somebody as no-account as me. Just some kid from some little town in the middle of the prairie. Dying was too big a thing for me. I wasn't important enough for it.

"Don't feel so good to be on the other end of the gun, does it Jesse?"

"Honest," I said, "I wasn't trying to kill you." My voice was hoarse and croaky. "Just trying to scare you some, so's you'd stop following me around."

"That a fact? Sure looked like you was aiming dead at me."

"I pulled aside. If I'd of wanted to kill you I wouldn't of missed, not from twenty feet."

He went on staring at me, but he didn't say anything, and I knew he was deciding about killing me.

"I brought your gun back. That's why I come." I couldn't bring myself to say I was sorry, even with that gun pointing at me. "I figured we could talk about it." I was froze up and my voice was whispery.

"That my gun there?"

I knew better than to pick it up. "It's your gun. I brought it back to show I wanted to be friendly." I tried to think of what else I could say to keep him from killing me. "Even Larry said you oughtn't to of been following me around," I said in my whispery voice.

He shifted a little on the log he was setting on. "I reckon you told Larry you was coming up here to see me."

Suddenly I saw he was worried about Larry. If I disappeared up here Larry'd have a mighty good idea I wasn't et by no mountain jack. "We talked it over. Larry said maybe he'd bring the gun back, but I told him no, it was my responsibility and I better do it myself." I paused. "I reckon he'll be glad to hear I done it and got back safe."

"Larry's gone soft on you," he said. "Stand up away from that gun." He hadn't decided about killing me. Maybe he'd go after Larry, too. I stood up.

"Move off to the side," he said.

I took a few steps to the right.

"Keep going till I tell you to stop." I stepped off ten feet.

"Okay," he said. "Set down right there." He jumped up and scooped the gun off the ground. "My gun all right."

"I was bringing it back to you so's maybe we could be more friendly."

He set back down on the tree trunk. "You know, Jesse, I've half a mind to shoot you where you sit. You took a shot at me, nobody would say nothing about it."

"Larry—"

"Burn your clothes, burn your hair off and the animals'd do the rest. Toss your belt buckle and your buttons in a lake somewhere and I'd be rid of you."

I was so froze I could hardly talk. But I wasn't going to beg. "Larry'd know," I kind of whispered. "He'd tell Pa. They all knew you killed a fella there in California." It was a risk saying that, but I had to chance it.

His face tightened, so did his hands on the gun. "That's a lie," he said.

"They all think so," I whispered.

He sat there staring at me, his face twisted up, his lips pulled back, his teeth clenched together. Wanted to kill me in the worst way, rip my clothes off'n me, pile them on my head and set them alight so's they'd burn the hair off me. Animals wouldn't eat hair.

Then his face smoothed out and he stood up. "I never shot a man in cold blood and I don't aim to do it now."

I felt so relieved I come near to crying. What was I going to say? That I was mighty grateful or something? I couldn't say that. But I knew I better say something. "I just hope we can be more friendly."

"I wouldn't shoot a boy. You tell Larry that."

"I will," I said. But he was lying. He'd of shot me all

115

right, but Larry would of known and told Pa, and maybe people'd come after him like they done in California.

"But on your part of it, you got to get out of my hair, Jesse. Go on back to town with your pa where you belong. I don't want you up here getting riled up and taking a shot at me no more. You hear, Jesse?"

I didn't want to promise to leave the mountain. He didn't have a right to ask that. I decided I wouldn't. "I hear," I said.

"I don't want you up here no more. You go on back to your pa. Don't waste no time about it. Understand?"

"I understand you," I said.

He jerked his head towards home. "Now you skeedaddle on out of here."

I didn't linger, but jumped off and set off through the woods as fast as I could go before he changed his mind, scrambling over fallen logs and rocks, wading through streams, until I was a good mile away from him. Then I eased off a little, found some blackberries the bears hadn't got to, ate them with my last biscuit and set off again. I was home before nightfall.

That night, after I ate my supper, I sat in front of my fire with my back resting against the cabin and thought about it. I didn't want to give up on being a mountain man, that was certain. I was beginning to get the hang of things up there. I was eating regular now, had got my cabin roofed in and the chimney started. I knew how to cure pelts and had got a half dozen ready to trade—rabbit, fox, one deerskin. A few more and I'd have enough pelts for some powder and lead, a bag of flour, a smoked ham. Meantime I'd get serious about cutting up a supply of wood for the winter. I wasn't a real mountain man yet, but I had a start on it. I didn't want to quit now.

What could Billings do to me? Maybe he'd come around and rough me up some. Punch me around. I didn't think he would, though, for if he done that I'd have a right to take a shot at him in self-defense. That was the law, they always said. Especially since he was a grown man and I was just a kid and couldn't defend myself against him otherwise.

What else could he do? I couldn't think of anything. Maybe it was all just talk. But I couldn't count on that, and I figured I better ask Larry about it. He would of wanted to know what happened, anyway. So the next afternoon I went around to see him. He'd got a bunch of pelts spread out in front of his cabin and was looking them over. "I reckon I'll go into the trading post in a day or so," he said. "How're you coming with your pelts?"

"I got three rabbits, two foxes, and a deer."

"It's a start," he said. He gave me a look. "You ever get up there to see our friend?"

"I never got there. He come across me first when I was snoozing."

"Oh?"

So I told him the whole story and he sat there listening. "What do you think he might do?"

Larry got up off the ground and sat down on the chopping block, squinting and thinking, the way he done. Finally he said, "From what you say, I reckon he don't get nothing from your pa until you go home."

"You don't think he's likely to rough me up?"

"He knows your pa wouldn't like that too good. He knows your pa wants you back in one piece, not all broke up."

"Then what can he do to me?"

"Oh, knowing Billings, I reckon he'll think of something."

There wasn't any more to say about it. I'd just have to wait and see. It wasn't much of a wait. Two mornings later when I went out to have a look at my snares, they was all sprung. Now a snare could get sprung—animal brush by it, branch drop on it. Could happen. But not all of 'em at once. Couldn't happen. Somebody come along with a stick and knocked 'em loose. It didn't take much thinking to figure out who that somebody was.

So I set the snares again, figuring he wouldn't pull the same stunt right away, but that's just what he done. Next day they was all sprung again. So I searched around and found another good spot for snares, a spring where two or three little animal trails come together. I set my snares there along the animal trails. I figure he'd find them sooner or later, but not right away. But blame if two days later they wasn't all sprung again. And I knew he was following me around—was probably out there in the woods that very minute watching me.

I stood there feeling cold and lonely. It was a bad feeling, knowing that somebody was out there somewheres laying for me. It wasn't just because Pa was going to give him something neither. He hated me, and would kill me if he dared. Maybe would kill me anyway, if he lost hold of himself the way I lost hold of myself and come near to killing him.

All of a sudden it come to me that maybe I ought to go into town and talk to Pa. I didn't want to, that was for certain. For one, I'd come near to killing him, and didn't know as I could face him over that. For another, I didn't want him thinking I couldn't take care of myself— handle Billings on my own. But the truth was, I *couldn't* handle Billings on my own. There was all sorts of ways he could hurt me—knock loose my snares, mess up my cabin when I was away, chop up my pelts, take some rocks off my roof so that the sheets of bark'd blow away. I had to get Pa to call Billings off. Oh, I didn't want to do it. I stood there for a while trying to think of some way to get out of it. But I couldn't: I had to do it. There wasn't no way around it.

I went on back to the cabin. I figured I might as well take my pelts down with me—tell Pa that was why I come. I ought to get some flour, bacon and such, especially if Billings was knocking loose my snares all the time. There wasn't no point in waiting around, so I bundled up the skins, hung them over my back, picked up my gun, and set off down the mountain.

It was coming up for rain. I hoped it'd hold off until I

got there. It rained the last time I went down, but I'd been looking for clouds that time. That wasn't more'n five, six weeks ago, but it seemed like years. So much'd happened since then and now. Helped kill a bear, got my cabin built, started to feel like a mountain man. Oh, a lot happened in that time. Didn't seem like I was the same person anymore. Different, somehow. I walked along through the trees trying to think how I was different. Come to see things clearer. See myself clearer, too, how I got ornery and such. When you're a kid you don't pay no attention to the things that happen around you. They just happen. But now I was taking a look at things a little more—what was the point of 'em, what did they mean?

Like learning to be a mountain man. I wasn't just learning how to put a roof on a cabin, cure a deerskin, salt down bear meat. I was *watching* myself learn them things. I was watching me turn myself into a mountain man. Seeing the progress I made, and after I got to where I could do something real good, looking back at the time when I couldn't do it at all. I'd come a long way since May. That little store down in town, with its old smells—tarry rope, lamp oil, new cloth—wasn't my home no more. The mountain was. I knew by the noises the crows were making that they'd found something dead I ought to look into in case the pelt was still worth something, knew from the smell of the wind when it was going to rain, knew from a tiny tuft of fur on a briar if a rabbit or fox had passed that way. The mountain was my home now, and I wanted to stay there forever. Pa was wrong: I wasn't going to get et by a mountain jack or freeze my behind off come winter.

I wasn't looking forward to seeing him, even so. Not so much about all them tools I took out of there five, six weeks ago. Pa wasn't going to trouble me about that. Didn't want to start a fight with me the first minute I turned up there. According to Larry, he wasn't going to make a fuss about busting him in the head neither. He'd let that slide, too, for now, anyway.

Why didn't I want to see him, then? Something to do with him wanting me back so bad. That was the part of it I never understood right from the time Larry told me about it. Here I'd busted him on the head, and then come back two, three weeks later and stole a heap of tools out of his store; and still he wanted me to come back. It didn't make no sense. What'd he want me back *for*? I didn't understand it, and it gave me a funny feeling.

By noon I was down on the prairie and plenty hungry. I was used to going hungry now and again, and I figured Pa would give me something to eat if I asked for it, so I didn't stop to search something up, but started off across the prairie. The wind had come up a little. It was going to rain soon enough. I hoped it'd hold off until I got into town. I picked up my pace a little, and after a while I began to see a line of low wooden buildings rise up out of the horizon. Some of them was painted up nice and shiny, yellow or brown, some just gray boards. I went on. The first drops of rain come as I hit the edge of town and began to walk along the boardwalk, passed the rows of houses set in their little yards—nice flower gardens in some of them, just a pack of weeds in others. Ahead I could see the steeple of the church. I began to trot and five minutes later I was standing on the walk across the street from Pa's store.

Blamed if I wanted to go in there. Just didn't want to see Pa, for whatever reason. But it was beginning to rain harder, and pretty soon it'd be just pouring. So I took a deep breath, walked across the street, up onto the store porch where Pa kept barrels of lamp oil, paint—stuff he didn't want getting slopped all over the floor inside. Now I was under the porch roof out of the rain and wasn't in such a rush to go inside. I took a quick peek through the window by the door. Pa had a couple of customers, and was behind the counter adding up some figures. I stood up against the wall out of sight of the windows and waited. Wasn't likely any new customers would come along until the rain quit. In a minute a fella come out carrying a sack of things. He gave me a glance but I didn't recognize him and he went trotting off through the rain. I stood there waiting some more, hearing the rain drumming on the tin porch roof, wishing I was back in my cabin, laying on my bed listening to the rain patter on the leaves and the stream rustle down the mountain, feeling nice and comfortable.

Then the other customer come out. He was someone I knew, but he didn't notice me tucked away against the wall. He made a face at the rain and trotted away. I took a deep breath and opened the door. The bell over the door jingled. Pa was behind the counter, head down, writing something in an account book. I stood by the door, waiting. Finally he finished writing and looked up.

Chapter Twelve

For a minute he didn't say anything, but just stared at me. Then he said, "So you finally came home."

"I ain't staying, Pa. I'm going back into the mountains. I reckoned we ought to talk." I could see a scar on the side of his head, where his hair ended by his ear.

He come out from behind the counter, through the boxes of soap and coffee, barrels of molasses. I watched him come. I didn't know what he had in mind—whack me one maybe. I didn't move. He put his arm around my shoulder and gave me a squeeze. "Well, I'm glad you come, even so, Jesse." He looked at my face. "I ain't had a look at you for a while. Looks like you toughened up some."

"I reckon I have, Pa." Blame me if I wasn't glad he put his arm around me and gave me a squeeze. I wasn't going to cry about it, though. "I figured I done some growing up the past couple of months."

He went on holding his arm over my shoulder. "Yes, I reckon you have." He took his arm off my shoulder. "Well," he said. I could see I took him by surprise and he wasn't sure how to talk to me. He looked at the store clock on the wall behind the counter. "Most likely you could use a little dinner right about now." He locked the door, and hung up the old sign saying CLOSED BACK IN AN HOUR. Then he gave my shoulders another squeeze. "I'm glad you came to see me, Jesse."

"I figured you might be sore at me for busting you on the head."

"Oh, I can't say I enjoyed it, but that's over the dam. Let's go upstairs."

We went on up. Pa melted some butter in a pan and started to break eggs into the butter. My, it smelt good. I hadn't touched a mouthful of eggs, much less butter, since I run off into the mountains. Blame me if it didn't feel good to be there. It was like coming home, except that it wasn't supposed to be my home no more. I broke away from it and didn't have no idea of ever living there again. And here I was setting there smelling them eggs and butter and feeling like I come home. It was all so familiar. Here was the yellow-painted table where I had my meals a thousand times. Ma painted that table herself when I was maybe four. I remember setting there watching that table turn from wood color to yellow bit by bit. There was the old iron stove I shook down and hauled the ashes out of twice a day for years, since I was old enough to carry a bucket of ashes, I reckoned. Get burnt on it more than once and run crying to Ma or Pa for them to put some grease on the burn. There was the funny chair with the drawer underneath the seat where the sewing things was kept—I remember Pa setting there often enough stitching up my shirt or pants where I ripped them. Ma must of sewed in that chair before Pa, but I didn't remember that. Oh, it was all so familiar, like I never left. Setting there, smelling them eggs cooking, my cabin up in the mountains seemed so far away. The whole thing was mighty confusing. I wished I didn't feel so much at home there. I wasn't being fair to my cabin. I know you couldn't be unfair to a cabin, but that's the way I felt.

Pa was slicing up some ham and bread to go along with the eggs. "Well, Jesse, how's it seem to be home again?" He was being careful how he put things.

"It's all right," I said. "I like it up there in the mountains pretty good, though."

He dropped the chunks of ham into the eggs to heat up. "You getting enough to eat, Jesse? You look a little on the thin side."

"Oh, I missed a meal here and there, but mostly I eat pretty regular," I said. "There ain't no shortage of game up there if you know where to look."

"You think you'll be able to get through the winter?"

"I reckon so," I said. "Them other fellas manage, I reckon I can, too." He was worried about me, afraid I might starve or freeze to death come winter. I reminded myself that it was him who put Billings onto springing my snares.

"Well, I hope so, Jesse. When a blizzard come it ain't like being here with a heap of coal laying in the back yard and plenty of food in the cupboard." He took a couple of tin plates off the shelf, loaded them up with eggs and ham, put down a plate of toast and a jar of jam in the middle of the table, and I dug in. It was mighty comfortable setting there shoveling all that grub in and watching through the window the rain fall into the Widow Wadman's backyard.

He didn't say much while I et, except how it looked like the rain was settling, or how the widow's calf broke loose the other day and et up half her cabbages before she could catch it. But every time I looked up from my plate he was watching me, not hardly eating himself, so when I was finishing he had to eat real quick to catch up.

Then he heated up the rest of his breakfast coffee, and we sat there drinking it—first cup of coffee I had in a good long while, too. I reckoned once I got set up good in the mountains I'd lay in some coffee. It tasted mighty good on a rainy day.

"Well, Jesse," he said. "I don't reckon you come down just for a visit. I reckon you got something on your mind."

All the way down I was thinking about what I was going to say. I didn't want to have a fight with him—was finished with that stuff. But I meant to stand up to him about this here Billings. "First thing, I'm real sorry I lost hold of myself and busted you with that pick handle. I shouldn't never of done it."

He shrugged. "I reckon I done a few things I hadn't ought to of done myself, Jesse. I reckon I lost my temper once too often with you, too. Maybe we ought to forget about what's past and start afresh."

I was bound and determined not to let him sweet-talk me into anything. "Pa, I don't reckon you knew it, but I always had my heart set on being a mountain man. It was the only thing I ever wanted to do."

He sat there thinking for a while. Then he said, "Well, I can see that. Them fellas coming in to the store with them big knives, looking hard as nails, telling them lies about dancing with the Indian girls and fighting bears with Bowie knives. I can see where it made keeping a store look mighty thin."

I was determined we wasn't going to have a fight. I was determined I'd keep a hold of myself. "They wasn't lies. I fought a bear with a knife myself."

He stared at me like he couldn't believe me. "You fought a bear with a knife?"

"Me and Larry. We shot him four, five times and didn't even slow him down. He went for Larry and I come up behind him, jumped on his back and started whacking at him with my knife." I remembered that musty smell and the dust rising off of his fur where the knife hit him. "The knife wasn't but a mosquito bite to him. Finally Larry shot him in the head." I took a deep breath to make sure I was keeping hold of myself. "It ain't lies."

"Well, all right," Pa said. "It sure sounded like lies."

"Larry danced with the Indian girls, too."

Pa looked at me. "You got to be pretty friendly with this fella Larry."

"Is there anything wrong with me having a friend?"

"No, no," he said. "Don't get riled up, Jesse. I'm glad you got somebody up there to keep an—to be friendly with."

I took a deep breath to get a hold of myself. "You got to have a friend up there. You got to have somebody to talk to from time to time or you start seeing things."

"You been seeing things?"

"No," I said. "But Larry, he got lost up there once and started to see Indians come waltzing down out of the sky."

"Don't know this here Larry real well. Know this fella Billings better. Larry come in here to trade from time to time, but he ain't real sociable. Likes to do his business and go on his way. This fella Billings, he'll set and chat."

Now we come of it. "Pa, I guess you know Billings is causing me a lot of grief."

He stared at me. "He is? What kind of grief?"

I looked back at him. "I figured you'd know."

He shook his head. "Why'd I know? How'd I know anything about it?"

"You put him up to it."

He wrinkled his brow. "I never done any such thing, Jesse. He tell you that?"

I didn't know where I was anymore. It wasn't like Pa to lie about a thing like that. But how else would you explain it? "Pa, you sure you never said nothing to him about running me off the mountain?"

"No. I wouldn't think of it. Not with Billings especially. Like I say, he's sociable enough, but the story is, he killed a couple of fellas out there in California. I wouldn't of wanted him to have nothing to do with you."

Now that I thought of it, I couldn't remember that Billings ever *had* said Pa'd put him on me. Couldn't remember exactly what he said, but as best I could recollect it wasn't that. Larry was the one who figured it out. Me and Larry together, anyway. "He's been following me around." I took a deep breath. "I took a shot at him. I lost hold of myself and took a shot at him. Only I pulled the muzzle at the last second."

Pa bent down to blow on his coffee. Then he turned his eyes up to look at me. "I knew that, Jesse."

That sure surprised me. "You knew it? How'd you know it?"

"Billings came down and told me. That's why I'm so blame worried about you."

I didn't say anything. Then I said, "He come down special to tell you?"

"I believe so. He said you was a risk to everybody up there and sooner or later somebody was bound to take a shot at you out of self-defense."

I felt mightily confused. "I figured you was behind it, Pa. I figured you was working together to get me down out of there."

He shook his head. "It wasn't me, Jesse. If he done anything, it was his own idea. What's he been doing?"

"Springing my snares. He's trying to starve me out."

Pa sat there thinking. Then he said, "I think he's dangerous, Jesse." I knew he wanted to say: come on home before you get hurt, but he knew that wasn't the way to handle me.

"But why? Why's he so all-fired up against me?"

"Jesse, some of these here mountain trappers are a little bit teched in the head. You got to be a little teched to live like that. Go off and live by yourself with nobody to talk to. No wife, no friends, no kiddies."

I hated hearing him talk like that. I felt myself starting to rile up and I took a deep breath. "Larry ain't teched."

"I didn't say all of 'em was. I don't know Larry so well as I could say. Don't know Billings so well neither, as far as that goes. But whatever he is, Jesse, you can't go around taking shots at people. You know that. Sooner or later you'll get yourself in real bad trouble. You got to learn to keep a hold of yourself."

Everything he said was right. I stopped feeling riled and looked down into my coffee. "I know that, Pa. I try. But sometimes I just can't help myself."

He leaned back and looked out the window. "You know, Jesse, when you was little, you was the nicest little boy anyone could ever want. Just as cute as a button. Just the smilingest little fella."

That surprised me, too. "I was?" It was hard for me to believe. "I don't remember that."

"Oh, you was. Everybody said so."

"People liked me?" The whole thing was surprising.

"Couldn't help but like you." He sighed. "Then you changed. I never could figure out what done it."

"Don't blame it all on Ma," I said. "I knew you was going to do that."

He looked at me and then he turned and looked out the window into the rain falling into Widow Wadman's yard. "I ain't blaming it all on your ma, Jesse. Not by a long shot. I had a hand in it. I guess I wasn't always the most sociable fella. Didn't always have control of myself neither. That's one reason why I took your ma out here from Pennsylvania. Couldn't get along with some of them back there. Spoke up too quick a few times. I figured I better make a fresh start. See if I couldn't learn to be more sociable."

He was having a time of it getting all of this out. Wanted to tell me, but was struggling with it. It made me feel not so riled up at him. "How come Ma said she'd come with you? She had all her family back there."

"She was young, just nineteen. I was a few years older, but pretty young myself. Back East we was always hearing stories about the West—the Rocky Mountains, cowboys and Indians, the fur hunters up in the mountains. To us—we hadn't much of a life to look forward to but working a farm somewheres—it sounded mighty exciting. Especially to your Ma. There was six kids in her family working a poor patch of land. For her it was hoeing corn, plucking chickens, washing dishes, scrubbing floors one day after the next. And if she married one of the local farmers it'd be more of the same, only worse, for she'd have her own babies to look after, too.

"The idea of going out West sounded mighty exciting to her. I had a little money set aside. We figured we'd find someplace where they needed a store. We'd see the Rockies, go to Indian dances, meet the cowboys, who knows, even discover gold or silver. We figured the town would grow and the store along with it, and after a while we'd be setting pretty. But it didn't work out that way. When they pushed the railroad through it went fifty miles to the north of us. Our town didn't grow—shrank a little, even, over time. We was hard-pressed to keep the store going. You have to sell on credit to the farmers until they get their crops in the fall and can pay you off, and if hard times come, drought or hailstorms that ruined the wheat, they wouldn't pay you at all, but sneak off farther West or give up and go back East. For your ma, it wasn't what she expected. She never figured on being snowed in for a week at a time with nobody to talk to but a little shaver and a husband who wasn't too sociable. She never figured on them dry spells in the summer when there was dust everywhere. Sweep and dust the house and by night-fall you could write your name with a finger in the dust on the tabletop. It wasn't no different for most wives out here. I worked on myself, learning to be more sociable. Go visiting folks with her when there was anyone to visit, set around in the evening and chitchat with her for a while. I done my best, but it wasn't my natural way. Back home there was six of 'em, always somebody to have a chitchat with, sing with when the work was dull, playing guessing games with, tell stories to. Back home she took all that for granted. Out here she missed it mighty bad. Finally the time come when she said she wanted to go home for a visit. But I knew she would never come back and I reckon she knew it, too."

"So it wasn't on account of me she left."

He looked me over real careful. "Think you can talk about it without taking another poke at me?"

"I reckon," I said.

"I wouldn't say you was the whole of it. I never did say that. Like I say, she was lonely, and seen nothing but blizzards, dust storms and loneliness stretching out before her. She was mighty blue about that. But you come into it. You was the thing that saved life for her. Cute as a button, a smile on your face all day long. Then you changed, fussing and feuding with us all the time. Never could figure it out."

I looked at him. "I don't remember anything about it, Pa. I never knew I was always smiling."

"It was what saved things out here for her. No matter how hard things got, she always had you, asetting there on the kitchen stool, laughing and talking a mile a minute while she cooked and sewed. She'd tell me about it in the evening, the funny things you said during the day, the little games you and she played together. It cheered her up mightily. But then you changed. You wasn't the nicest little boy anyone could ever want anymore. She seen the way you was going and she couldn't stand it. She said it was breaking her heart."

"But it wasn't all my fault, was it, Pa?"

"No. But you come into it, Jesse."

I didn't say anything for a minute. Then I said, "Why'd you have to say that to me, Pa?"

"You ain't a little kid no more, Jesse. Someday you got to learn that if you act ornery with folks it's bound to come bouncing back on you."

Chapter Thirteen

I sat there staring down at the tin plate in front of me, smeared up with egg yolk and scraps of ham growing cold. The rain drummed in my ears, and slowly things began to come back to me, things I completely forgot for years. I remembered her crouched down with her arms around me, holding me tight and crying, "Jesse, oh Jesse, why do you do these things? Whatever am I going to do with you?" Crying to beat anything so my face was wet with her tears, and me standing there stiff as a board in her arms. What had I done? I couldn't remember, but it must have been something.

I remember me running around the backyard with her chasing me, ducking and dodging so's she couldn't catch hold of me, and her crying out, "Jesse, oh Jesse, you're going to drive me crazy, I swear you will." What had I done that time? I couldn't remember that neither.

I remembered other things, just scraps and pieces, where Ma had got hold of me and was whacking my tail and crying, "Jesse, I can't stand doing this to you anymore, I can't stand it, I can't stand it," and me standing there straight and stiff while she whacked me. "What's got into you, Jesse? What in Heaven's name has got into you?"

What had? I don't know. But one thing was clear: I'd hit Pa with the axe handle because I couldn't stand hearing the truth of it.

I sat there feeling rotten—cold and empty inside, like I wasn't no use to anybody including myself and might just as well throw myself away. I squeezed my eyes shut to get rid of them memories. I reckoned that's why I forgot them in the first place—didn't want to think of what I was doing to Ma. I looked at Pa. He seemed different to me all of a sudden. Not so fierce. More like a person who had his good side and bad side, and probably been hurt a few times hisself. I shut my eyes again for a couple of seconds. "I can remember Ma crying over me, but blamed if I can remember what I done."

"You done near everything a little kid could do. Just get in a state and go wild. Throw stuff through windows. Dump your dinner on the floor. Start hitting at us. All kind of things."

"What made me do it, Pa? I wouldn't of done it for no reason."

He shook his head. "Blamed if I could ever figure it out. You'd go along peaceable for a while and then it'd take hold of you again. Never knew what it was. The funny thing was, after your ma left it got better. You'd fly off the handle sometimes, throw things around, but it wasn't so bad as it was before she left. I generally got you calmed down before you did too much damage."

That struck me mighty strange. "I was better after she left?"

137

"Well, it seemed strange to me, too. It was like you had it in for her, for some reason. I never understood it."

I sat there trying to make sense of it. "You never knew where Ma went to? Never heard nothing about her?"

"About three months after she left I got a letter. She said she wasn't coming back, she couldn't stand the prairie no more, and besides, she wanted to be near her folks—pa and ma, all them brothers and sisters. She said she got a job in Erie, which wasn't too far from her folks' farm. Clerking in a grocery store, which she learned out here. She said she didn't have no way to keep you yet, but would send for you when she got things worked out better."

"She couldn't of kept me?"

"How was she gonna look after you when she was working all day, six days a week? You wasn't but seven years old then."

"Why couldn't I of lived on the farm with her folks?"

"They was getting on, Jesse. I don't reckon they was ready to take on no seven-year-old kid, not after raising six theirselves. Anyway, knowing them, they wouldn't of encouraged it. They'd of said her place was with her husband." He stopped and looked out the window at the rain falling onto the Widow Wadman's tin roof. "If you want to know the truth of it, Jesse, I reckon she was waiting till she could find herself a husband. Mighty hard for a lone woman to raise a child if she ain't got somebody to look after it while she works."

"You don't think she ever found a husband?"

138

"I figure she did. A couple of years later I got this letter from some lawyer in Erie. Said she wanted a divorce. I figured she got herself a fella."

"Why didn't she ask for me then? Was it because I was too ornery?" I hated thinking that.

"Jesse, I don't know as we ought to go into all of that. I reckon we ought to let all them things lie."

But I couldn't let them lie; they was itching and scratching at me too much. I couldn't stand thinking Ma didn't want me just because I was ornery sometimes. There had to be another reason. "I got a right to know, Pa."

"I can't rightly answer, Jesse. Maybe the fella didn't like kids. If there was any such fella. Maybe she felt bad about running off and couldn't face you and me. I reckon we ought to let all this lie."

I could see it hurt him to talk about it, but I was getting stubborn. I wanted to know, no matter how it hurt. "Pa, you got to tell me. I got a right to know why she didn't send for me."

He seen I was getting riled up and had better answer before I stomped off out of there. "All right, Jesse, but you ain't gonna like it."

"I don't care."

He sat there thinking for a minute. Then he said, "I wrote this here Erie lawyer a letter saying that she could have the divorce, if she didn't want to live with me I didn't care to be married to her no more. But I was keeping the boy. I wasn't gonna give you up."

139

"What'd she say?"

"She didn't say nothing," Pa said. "All I got was a letter from the lawyer saying your ma agreed I could have you, provided I fork over for her lawyer. Two hundred dollars. I said I'd pay."

"You mean she could have had me back? Could have come out here and took me away with her?"

"I'd have fought her, Jesse," he said. "Would have gone to court and told the judge she'd had her chance to you, she'd left of her own accord. Don't know how it would have come out. Maybe she figured she couldn't win."

"She could have tried."

"I told you, you wasn't gonna like it, Jesse. Who knows, maybe this fella didn't want to raise no other man's child." He shrugged. "Hard to know. Maybe the lawyer talked her into it. Figured the only way he was gonna get paid was get the money out of me."

"And you done it, Pa?"

"Yes, I done it, Jesse. I wanted to keep you."

I sat there staring down into the plate with the egg smears and scraps of ham, feeling confused, wound up tight. The whole world had changed for me in half an hour. I wanted to throw something, but I knew I wasn't supposed to do that no more. I looked up at him. "Why'd you want to keep me, the way I was losing hold of myself all the time? That don't make no sense."

He shrugged again. "Made enough sense to me."

"Where'd you get the two hundred dollars?"

"Took a loan from the bank," he said. "They was willing to give it to me, because I had the store and was probably good for it. Spent two years paying it off, ten dollars a month."

I sat quiet, hurting real bad. "Maybe this fella didn't want me around. Maybe she couldn't help it." I looked at him. "You figure for sure she got married?"

"Don't know for sure. Most likely. Could have a couple of kids by now."

That hadn't even crossed my mind. I jumped up. "Kids? She might have other kids besides me?"

"Calm down, Jesse. You wouldn't be the first one who had brothers and sisters."

I could see the truth of that, but it didn't help much. I couldn't stand the idea of Ma saying, "The boy stood on the burning deck" to some other kid when she tucked him in bed. I shook my head to get rid of the picture. "Maybe she didn't have no more kids besides me. Maybe this fella didn't like any kind of kids."

"Could be," Pa said.

I sat down. "I got to find out. I got to write her a letter."

"Jesse, we got no idea where she's at."

"This here Erie lawyer's bound to know."

"She could of moved two, three times since then," Pa said.

I thought about it for a minute. "I'm going to find her. Maybe someday I'll go back East and find her. I know where her folks live, the little town she come from."

He shrugged once more. "You'll be a grown man

soon, Jesse. You can do what you want. I ain't fighting you."

I looked back at him. "Don't worry, I ain't gonna lose a hold of myself."

"If you learned that out of it, it was worth it. The way you was going you was bound to get yourself in serious trouble."

I was beginning to feel itchy and scratchy inside. "Don't worry, Pa, I won't bring no trouble down on you."

He stood there staring at me. The rain was still drumming on the roof. "Jesse, is that what you think? The only reason it'd matter to me if you got in trouble was that it'd come down on me?"

I didn't want him trying to get nothing like that across to me. "I don't see what else it'd be."

He leaned towards me a little to look in my face. "Jesse, sometimes I could just weep for you. Don't you see that somebody might care for you, as ornery as you are? Don't you see how much your ma must of cared for you to run away from you when she seen how you was headed?"

I winced, like he hit me. "I don't need nobody to take care of me. I can take care of myself."

He went on looking at me, like I was a stranger he was trying to figure out. Then he said, "Maybe that's your trouble right there. I got to open up the store." He picked up the dishes off the table and put them in the sink.

"You don't need to do that," I said. "I'll wash the dishes."

"All right," he said. "What do you plan to do now?"

"Go back up to the mountains, I reckon."

"Well, look, Jesse, it's getting dark and raining still. Best sleep here in your own bed tonight and get a fresh start in the morning. It's nice for you to have some company for a change."

And burnt up as I was, and scratchy inside, blame if I didn't want to stay.

Chapter Fourteen

It felt kind of strange climbing into my old bed after all them weeks, but homey, too. I got that snug feeling you get when the rain's beating on the roof and the night is closed in tight around you. Blame comfortable, too, after sleeping on that plank bed I made for myself in the cabin. I wasn't tempted to come back to it, snug as it was, for I liked it up in the mountains too much to come back. But there wasn't no harm in it once in a while.

In the morning I had a cup of coffee and some toast with Pa. "You need anything, Jesse?" he asked. "You need anything, just go down to the store and take it. No need to come sneaking in a window in the dead of night."

I blushed. It was the first he'd mention them tools I took. It seemed like I managed to do everything wrong. But I wasn't going to take anything from him. "I brought down some pelts. I can pay my own way. If you could sell them I'll take it out in trade next time I come down."

"I'll see what I can get for them." He stood up and so did I. "Take care of yourself, Jesse." He put his hand on my shoulder and gave it a little squeeze. "No matter what you think, I wouldn't be too happy if something happened to you."

I knew I ought to say something nice to him, but like always, I was having trouble with it. "I guess I'll be all right," I said. Then I said, "Maybe I'll come down again and say hello in a while."

So I picked up my gun and went back into the mountains. It eased my mind some to be walking up there amidst the oaks, maples, hemlocks, birches and the rest, the birds twittering and flashing around and the little animals scurrying away across the dried leaves and twigs. But I had a power of things on my mind that kept swirling around in my head. For one thing, Billings. Pa'd said he never set Billings on me, and I believed him. Why was Billings so fired up to get me off the mountain? Just hated kids, the way Larry said? Was a little teched, like Pa figured? Maybe just plain liked hurting people—scaring them, springing their snares, maybe even killing them like he done out in California. I couldn't figure it, but he was trouble, that was certain.

Then there was Ma. I couldn't make no sense out of that at all. I couldn't believe I'd forgot all them times I gave her grief. They was clear enough in my mind now, that was certain—her clutching me and weeping and me struggling to get loose from her. How could anyone forget such things as that? But they'd slipped right out of my mind, probably right after they happened, and stayed slipped out for years. If you wanted to forget about things, it seemed like you could. I don't reckon any kid would want to remember giving his ma that kind of grief and would forget it if he could.

I went on walking up the mountain, not paying much attention to the birds twittering through the air and the squirrels going *crek-crek-crek* the way I usually done, but remembering things; remembering Ma coming in with a jar full of wildflowers on the prairie—saying, "Jesse, don't they look just grand, they cheer up the room so." And as soon as her back was turned I took her scissors and chopped the heads off the flowers and flung them out the window. Why on earth did I do that to Ma? I remembered throwing salt in the sugar bowl, I remembered dumping her sewing basket onto the floor so all the little spools of thread ran every which way across the floor. Why did I do these things? Getting even with Ma, it seemed like.

I saw I'd go crazy if I went on thinking about it, so I made myself listen to the birds and look around at things the way I usually did, taking it all in, noticing things, like a deer trail or a berry bush I didn't notice before. And I was going along like that when there came into my mind the picture of a field of tall grass, hayfield maybe, bent over the wind, the picture that always made me feel so bad. Here it came again, the skin going tight over my head, stomach knotting up. I stopped walking and stood still, waiting for it to end. But this time I got hold of something I never saw before: the picture had something to do with Ma. I closed my eyes to see it better. I was once again in that shed or barn all by myself, looking across the field of grass half hid in the shadows of it. What was she doing? My eyes closed, I stared as hard as I could into those woods. It was Ma all right, but I couldn't see what she was doing. "Ma, what is it?" I whispered.

But there wasn't no answer, and after a while I give myself a big shake like a dog coming out of water, and started on up the hill again, feeling a little more comfortable with myself.

I had got pretty far up into the mountains and was coming into my own territory, maybe a half mile from the cabin, when I smelled smoke. A wood fire somewhere. Somebody out cooking hisself some dinner, maybe. Wasn't usual, though. Who'd it be? Larry wouldn't be cooking nothing out in the middle of the woods, not when he was half an hour from home. Might be Billings, but it didn't seem likely he'd give hisself away like that. I lifted my nose and took a sniff. Just wood smoke, no smells of meat frying.

A little breeze come down the mountains towards me, and now I saw a faint grayness drifting through the woods. I tipped my head back to smell again. There was more smoke blowing through the upper branches of the trees in big clumps. It wasn't no cooking fire.

All at once I knew what it was and I started to run through the trees as hard as I could, bumping and tripping here and there on trees and rocks, trying to hold the gun so it wouldn't catch on nothing. I ran on, and then I began to see through the trees flame flickering orange and smoke rising up heavy. I was going to be too late.

I busted out into the cabin clearing. The flames had got the cabin near buried. They was rising twenty feet over the roof, the smoke streaming upward and then breaking apart as the breeze caught it and blew it off through the trees down the mountainside. I only cut them logs a month ago and they was mostly still green. He must of flung oil all over it before he set it alight. Green wood didn't start easy, but once it got going it burned hotter than dry. I was going up good now, crackling and snapping and sending off showers of sparks when something popped.

I ran up to the door and looked in through the flames. Couldn't see nothing but smoke and fire, but I reckoned he took the tools out first. Wouldn't of wanted good tools to go to waste. Then I remembered I left the axe leaning against the back wall. I ran around behind. The wall was covered with flames, but I could see well enough that the axe was gone.

The funny thing was, I didn't lose hold of myself. Instead I went cold and clear in my mind. I was going to shoot him dead, no question about that, and do it in the next half hour. I stopped to figure. He'd of stuck around, set down back up the woods where he could see the cabin to make sure it was burning good. He wasn't no more'n fifteen, twenty minutes ahead of me at most. He was carrying a whole load of tools—axe, saw, pick, nails, whatever else I had there. He'd of had to take time to rope all that stuff around him. Loaded down like that he wouldn't be traveling too fast. He might not be more'n five, ten minutes away. I'd catch him quick. Then he was going to be dead, dead, dead, laying there in the woods amongst the trees on his back, his arms stretched out, bleeding out of his head where the bullet went in. Oh, I couldn't hardly wait.

But I knew I had to be cold about it. Which way'd he gone? Uphill out of the smoke, for one. Probably carted all the stuff out of the cabin, laid it up there somewhere, come back, tossed oil all over the cabin, set it on fire, then come back to where he laid the tools and set there waiting until the fire was going good.

I started to move as fast as I could up the mountain through the trees and over the rock outcroppings. I hadn't gone but a hundred yards when I saw a place on the ground under the trees where the leaves and needles was kicked up some. I crouched down and had a look. I saw a heel mark in the ground, and a little slit in the ground, too, about four, five inches long and an inch deep, with a little chunk out of one edge of the lip. I seen marks like that before: axe blade was dropped there. Fella wouldn't stick an axe in the ground on purpose—take the edge off the blade mighty quick that way. But he'd been in a rush—took those tools out of the cabin and just dropped them up here, and by accident the axe landed on the blade, dug in a little, and then fell over sideways, pulling loose a little chunk of dirt. I looked down toward the cabin. I could see the flames well enough here. He hunkered down on his heels watching until he was sure it was burning good.

I stood up and took a look at the ground around me. It didn't take me more than a minute to see which direction he'd gone in. All those tools bundled around him was catching at branches and twigs as he pushed through. Most of them would snap back as he went by, but some would break. I wasn't going to have much trouble following him.

I stood there for a minute listening, for I figured them tools was bound to bump into each other and clink. I didn't hear nothing, so I set off again, ducking and dodging through the branches of the trees. There was another advantage I had: I was a foot shorter than he was and could duck under branches he had to push through or walk around. I'd catch him sooner or later. I went on, stopping here and there to listen for a clink. All the while my mind stayed clear and cold, and I could see him sprawled out among the trees, his arms spread, blood leaking out of a hole in his head. I'd pile his clothes over his head and burn his hair off, like he was going to do to me; and by tomorrow there wouldn't be nothing left of him.

Then I heard what I was waiting for—a soft clink up there ahead of me somewheres. My innards began to dance, for now I knew I had him. I stood still and listened. There come another clink. He was maybe a couple of hundred yards ahead of me, up to the north going in the direction of his own territory. I wanted to take him from the uphill side. I had to follow him along until I got to a place where the woods thinned out a little so's I had a clear shot at him from someplace hidden. Wanted to make sure I had time to take careful aim and kill him right off.

I turned west, up the mountainside, going as quick as I could without making no noise. When I got up in there fifty yards I set off north again, running parallel to the direction he was going. From time to time I heard that little clink—probably when a branch slapped the axe or pick against the shovel. Something like that. He wasn't in any rush—figured it wasn't likely I even knew my cabin was burnt down yet.

Then the clinks stopped. I listened. Nothing. What'd he done? Had he heard me coming along behind me and was hunkered down, waiting? I crouched down low amongst the trees and looked downhill, moving my eyes slow and careful over the whole woods there. Nothing —no funny lump or shadow down amongst the leaves and branches.

I turned my head off to the left. The woods thinned out there—some kind of clearing maybe. Good place to get a look around. I raised up a little and scooted along low to the ground until I come to the edge of the woods. I dropped flat into the leaves.

In front of me was a little grassy glade, maybe fifty yards across, pretty little spot, with the sun shining on the grass and the woods beyond. And across the other side sat Billings, his back against a tree at the edge of the woods over there, where he'd be out of the sun. The tools were scattered on the ground around him, and he was munching on something—piece of my salt meat, I reckoned. I had him now.

We'd been moving along for near an hour now. Probably covered something like four miles. He figured he was safe: even if I discovered the fire by now, there wasn't much chance I'd ever find him. He could take it easy.

He was getting sideways to me, his legs sprawled out in front of him, his gun across his lap. One hand laid on the gun, the other was holding the food up to his face. Made a good target all right—couldn't have asked for nothing better. I pulled back into the woods, and checked the gun over real good. Didn't want no misfire. You could hear a misfire click a hundred yards away when the woods was quiet.

I wasn't feeling so cold and clear anymore. Nervous and excited, sort of a light, jittery feeling. But I wasn't loosing ahold of myself neither. I was thinking clear enough, and I thought it through. Wanted to make sure I hurt him real bad on the first shot, even if I didn't kill him. It'd take me maybe thirty seconds to reload. If I caught him in the neck, or busted his shoulder, arm or something, it'd take him a little bit to get himself pulled together to the point where he could start looking around for me. The main thing was make sure I hit him somewhere. I calculated that if I aimed just a little over his head, the ball would drop enough over fifty yards to catch him in the head somewheres; and if it dropped more it'd get him in the neck, shoulder, something.

I checked the gun once more, and then I slid forward until I was at the edge of the woods. I was tensed up pretty good and feeling light in my muscles, but still thinking clear. For a bit I looked down across the grassy glade, all covered with sun to where he was sitting. There he was, his teeth clenching down on that meat, his stomach pushing against his belt when he breathed in and out, the sweat drying on his face. And in thirty seconds, a minute maybe, he wasn't going to be nothing but a heap of dirt. It seemed amazing to me how you could turn a living, breathing person into nothing in a second. One second chewing away, that piece of meat tasty in his mouth, and the next second nothing.

I was still far enough back in the woods to be in the shadows. I wanted to move forward a little to get out of the patchy light there. I slid on my belly, never for a minute taking my eyes off Billings fifty yards away across the grass glade. Behind me I heard a quiet rustle of leaves and felt a little breeze blow across me. The breeze spread down into the glade, brushing the grass like a hand running over a cat's fur. That old feeling come over me. My stomach tensed up, the hair tightened on my scalp, my guts grew cold and cramped. I began to sweat. I knew I better shoot before it took me. I raised the gun and sighted, the bead just a fraction above Billings' hair. The cramp in my guts come on strong, hurting me. I started to squeeze the trigger.

Then I realized I wasn't seeing Billings no more. I was

seeing Ma. She was setting on a log at the edge of the woods, her legs stretched out in front of her. Sitting next to her was a fella I never seen before—tall fella with yellow hair. He'd got his legs stretched out, too. She had her hand on his arm and was smiling up into his face. He was smiling down on her, too, and as I watched she raised up her head to kiss him.

I sucked in a big gasp of air and then lay there frozen, still staring down the barrel of the gun into the woods. My head was dizzy, and my heart was going a mile a minute. I shuddered, and sucked in another gasp of air, and then slowly I began to unfreeze. For a moment I went on laying there, not thinking of anything, but just going slowly soft, like a balloon that the air was leaking out of. Then it come to me that Billings might spot me, and I crawled back into the woods where I'd be in the shadows. I lay there for the longest while, staring up through the branches to the bits and pieces of sky I could see through the leaves, as if I'd finally got myself loose after I'd been knotted up for years and years.

Chapter Fifteen

The sun was going down behind the mountain and the woods was filling up with shadows, like water rising in a pool. Larry had got a fire going and was sizzling a big chunk of venison in his frying pan, poking it around with his knife so as to cook it even all around. Down next to the coals biscuits was baking in his covered cast-iron pan. "And you don't have no idea who that fella with your Ma was?"

"No. Didn't recognize him, anyway. I wasn't but five, six years old then. Could have been some fella passing through for all I know. Or it could have been the one she wanted to marry later on. Went off with him one night and they got married later on. Could have been somebody else altogether. Don't know one way or another."

"You ain't sore at your Ma for it?"

"That's the funny thing, Larry. I ain't sore at her. Reckon I ought to be, but I ain't. Ain't sore at nobody for a change. Kind of like I was set free of that. Still ain't sure where it happened. Ain't no woods or grassy place like that on the prairie. There's places like that along the river, back by the trading post. Could have been over there. Most likely was. She went over there to meet this fella and had to take me along for some reason. Usually she would of left me with Widow Wadman when she had to go somewheres. But maybe she had it planned, and Widow Wadman took sick and she had to take me along with her. Don't know. That's the best I can guess. And they put me to sleep there in some shed and went off away where she could talk to this fella, but close enough so's she could hear me cry if I woke up. Then I woke up, looked out the door, window, and seen them. Something like that. But maybe it wasn't like that at all. I'd sure like to find out."

Larry looked at me with that squinty look he got sometimes. "Jesse, maybe I shouldn't say this, but are you sure it really happened? Wasn't some kind of a dream or something?"

I shook my head. "No, it happened. How could I get my guts all clawed up like that over a dream?"

"Dreams is funny things."

"No," I said. "It happened. I learned something else —you can forget things if they're troublesome to you. I forgot all them things I used to do until I got to talking about them to Pa. I reckon this was the same—too troublesome to remember."

He nodded. "Maybe so. Billings come out of it mighty lucky, I'll say that. You, too, far as that goes."

"Why me?" I said. "I had a right to kill him."

"Maybe so," Larry said. "But you'd of found it a hard thing to live with. Killing a fella ain't nothing you shrug off the next day. Most fellas, anyway."

"I don't know. I still don't know why he was so fired up to get me."

"Probably won't ever know," Larry said. "Like your pa says, most likely he's a little teched in the head. Some fellas just plain like to give people trouble. They're funny that way. Only thing is to stay clear of them. But I don't think you'll have no more trouble with him. He knows you took a shot at him once and might do it again. He knows you know it was him burnt down your cabin. He'll stay clear of you."

"I wouldn't mind that," I said. "I don't want to see him come walking into the store."

"I don't reckon he will." He paused. Then he said, "You figure on going back down there?"

"I reckon so. I got a lot of things to figure out for myself. Got to get a hold of myself, get a fresh start. For one, I need some more schooling. How'm I going to write to Ma if I can't spell?"

"You aiming on writing her?"

"Yes. I got to find out about it. It'll prey on me if I don't."

"Suppose you can't find her? Suppose that lawyer don't know where she's at?"

"Go look for her someday soon. She's got all them brothers and sisters back there in Pennsylvania. One of them's bound to know where she's at."

"Maybe she didn't go back there. Maybe she went out to California or something."

"Somebody back there'll know. She was always talking

about them. Kept up with them as best she could."

"What'll you do if you get a hold of her?" Larry said.

"Find out. That's all. Find out things. Why she done it and all. Tell her I seen her with that fella but I ain't sore at her."

He gave the frying pan a shake. "This here deer meat's near done." He took the frying pan off the fire and laid it next to the coals to keep warm. "Them biscuits need a couple minutes more," he said. He gave me a kind of sideways look. "I don't expect you'll be telling your pa about that fella?"

"No, I don't expect so. Maybe he knows and wouldn't never say anything about it to me."

"Could be. You figure you can get along with your pa a little better now, Jesse?"

"I believe so. I see him more plain now. Oh, I reckon we'll always scrap some. He ain't so different from me. Ornery. But I reckon we can manage."

"Well, Jesse, you had yourself a mighty hard three, four months. That's certain. If you learned something out of it, maybe it was worth it."

"I guess so," I said. "I ain't exactly sure what I learned yet, but I must of learned something. Learned one thing for certain—you can't get away from people by going off into the mountains. They was all inside of me, anyway."

"Looks like it, don't it?" Larry said. "Well, I'm gonna miss having you drop around from time to time. I have to admit it. Ornery as you was, you was good company."

"Oh, I'll come up and see you now and again, Larry.

Don't worry about that. Don't doubt but what I'll get itchy and scratchy down there from time to time and I'll want to come up for a breath of fresh air. Reckon I might come up here and build another cabin one of these days when I get bigger. Can't say for certain, but I kind of got used to it up here. Got an interest to it you don't have in town. Don't figure I'd of fought a bear with a knife down there."

"Don't figure you want to do it again neither, Jesse, down there or up here."

I grinned. "I expect not. But I'm glad I done it once."

He touched his hand to the top of the cast-iron pan. "I reckon them biscuits is done. Let's eat."